Tales from the Second Great War

1940 – 1941

A Misfit Squadron Book

Simon Brading

First published 2020

This edition published 2024

ISBN: 978-1-917470-05-6

ENGLAND EXPECTS

ENGLAND EXPECTS

England, 12th September 1940

From ten thousand feet there was a truly lovely view of the white cliffs, shining in the bright sunlight, and Chastity took a split second to appreciate it, her eidetic memory storing it away for later perusal, as she approached the apex of the loop her Spitsteam was describing and hung inverted in the sky. It wasn't just the landscape she took in in that brief moment, though, but the entirety of the battle going on above the busy port nestled in a break in the cliffs.

92 Squadron had been sent up to intercept a sizeable Prussian raid, on its way to bomb Dover, and while a Harridan squadron, she forgot which one, was doing its best to take care of the forty or fifty Hoffman HO111's, the Spits had been left to scrap with the MU9's. As usual.

As the battle had progressed, she had somehow become separated from the rest of her squadron and found herself fighting for her life against two pairs of Fleas. The two pairs had competed for firing position on her, getting in each other's way, and in the chaos she had managed to get in a few of shots, shooting down one and forcing another away, evening the odds slightly, but the last two were proving to be quite tenacious and, try as she might, she couldn't get them off her tail.

She craned her neck to look back around the loop as far as she could. Just creeping into view above the armour plate at the rear of the cockpit were the enemy fighters. The wingman was still tucked in right behind his leader, despite the dizzying ride she had taken them on, and she didn't really need to see the red noses of their machines to know that they were veterans of more than just the battle over Britain. However, it wasn't just their skill that was making her life difficult, but also the fact that they were flying the "F" variant of the MU9, which had come into production only recently. It had improved aerodynamics, a more powerful spring, and, instead of having its cannon in its wings, they had been fitted into the nose along with two machine guns and fired through the propeller. It all combined to make them far more deadly than the "E" variants the British were used to facing and her ageing Spitsteam was definitely outclassed.

All was not lost, though, and she wasn't going to have to try to disengage yet, because she still had a few tricks up her flightsuit sleeve - like the knowledge that the MU9F had a slightly higher stalling speed than the Mark I Spitsteam.

That was why she'd led the Fleas on a very long and very basic loop - she'd been forcing them to slow down and was hoping that they'd be too greedy for the kill to notice what was happening until it was too late.

She kept her eyes fixed on the aircraft of the leader, knowing it would have to come soon, otherwise the loop would be done and they'd be able to fire on her.

There!

It was minimal, a minute twitch as first the leader's machine, then the wingman's, expressed its displeasure and discomfort at its pilot's handling, but to Chastity it was as obvious as if they had sent up an emergency flare.

The pilots finally realised what was happening and deployed flaps, but it was too late; Chastity was already moving. She snapped the Spitsteam onto its wing and let the nose drop below the horizon to pick up speed, even as she pulled the stick back into her lap.

The enemy machines opened fire but it was a desperate move and the shots missed by, almost literally, a mile as they stalled and completely lost control of their aircraft.

As the Spitsteam accelerated, the G forces piled on, but Chastity screamed her defiance at the approaching darkness and didn't allow it anywhere near her.

The enemy aircraft were picking up speed as they dropped from the sky and would soon regain enough speed for their wings to bite once more, but they had run out of time and, before the two falling rocks could become aircraft again, Chastity found the dot of her reflector sight squarely over the wingman. She pressed the button on the stick, putting a two-second burst into him and was treated to the spectacle of the starboard side wing folding up and smashing the cockpit before the aircraft spun away. The leader wandered into her sights next, but he had recovered somewhat and was diving away desperately. She was only able to give him a half second burst before she could no longer keep the red dot over him, though, and she rolled the Spitsteam onto its back again, keeping the stick in her lap, and followed...

'...him down to the sea. He must have been damaged or hurt, though, because he barely manoeuvred once we were there and a couple more shots put him straight in.'

The intelligence officer, Aviator Lieutenant Barbara Yarrow, made a note on the pad of paper on the table in front of her, before looking up again. 'Anyone around to see?'

'We were still in sight of the cliffs, so the Observer Troop must have seen us. There were also plenty of boats around if they didn't.'

'I'll get on to the Troop and see what they have to say, although things got quite busy over Dover and they might have missed it. And where was Porter in all of this?'

'He had spring trouble right after we took off.'

The prim and proper sixty-year-old woman gave Chastity a shrewd look, but said nothing and just made another note on her pad. 'Anything else to report? Did you see anyone bag anything?'

Chastity shook her head. 'No, I was too busy and far away from the main scrap to see much.'

'Very well.' Yarrow capped her pen and stood. 'That will be all, then. Thank you, Arrowsmith.'

'Thank you, ma'am.'

Chastity waited for the officer to precede her from 92 Squadron's dispersal hut before going out into the sunshine.

She shaded her eyes to gaze around the airfield. Despite having been the focus of so many enemy raids and being one of the busiest air bases in England, Biggin Hill was extremely calm and picturesque, on top of a hill and surrounded by trees and fields, with a sleepy village right next to it. The only real sign of urgency to the day was the fitters swarming over the lines of parked aircraft like ants, continuing their eternal fight to turn them around before the enemy came back.

As one of the most junior pilots, she was the last to give her report and the other pilots were already out with their tea and snacks. A few were lazing around in deck chairs or sitting on the grass, but most were in a group, perched on the few tattered sofas and armchairs that looked like they had been rescued from a bombed-out house. She wandered over to the mess van parked between the dispersal hut and the line of aircraft, got a cup of tea and a plate of biscuits from the NAACI volunteer, then came back and made her way over to where the only other female pilot in the squadron, Roberta Collingwood, was sitting on the grass, leaning back on her elbows with her face tilted to the sun. There were still too many men in the armed forces who thought that a woman didn't belong on the battlefield and a lot of them seemed to be in the squadron, so the two of them stuck together, as much out of solidarity as friendship, and consoled each other every time a man who'd been in the RAC less time than them was promoted past them.

'Berty.' Chastity nodded at the woman then sat down next to her.

Collingwood squinted at her through heavily lidded eyes. 'Chas.'

Chastity offered her plate. 'Biscuit?'

'Ta.' Collingwood pushed herself upright and took one of the Bourbons, her favourites, which Chastity had gotten specifically for her. She had dark hair, almost the same shade as Chastity's, but it was there that all similarity ended. While Chastity could only charitably be described as good-looking, Roberta Collingwood was stunning, with a perfect complexion and lips that Chastity had heard one of her boyfriends describe as "succulent". Unfortunately, that just meant that she was treated even worse by many of the pilots than Chastity herself was, because she refused to return any of their clumsy, and usually drunk, advances.

They munched on the biscuits in silence for a minute or so, watching the pilots around them. A few had sensibly fallen asleep, getting whatever rest they could, but the group on the sofas were laughing and talking loudly. Aviator Lieutenant William Porter, Chastity's leader, was among them and as always was the loudest.

Chastity swallowed her mouthful and washed it down with tea, then looked away from the distasteful sight of Porter holding court.

'Did you hear?' Collingwood said excitedly. 'The Misfits met a raid over the Midlands yesterday evening and bagged themselves twenty-seven.'

Chastity grunted, curling her lip disdainfully. She was sick and tired of hearing about the successes of the rejects of the so-called *Misfit Squadron*, who had somehow gone from being a laughing stock to mythical heroes, even after their failure in France. 'That's absurd! They only have eight fighters, there's no way they shot down that many. The numbers are being inflated for morale, trust me.'

Collingwood shrugged, her enthusiasm not at all dimmed. 'Even if they only got half that, it's more than everyone in our squadron put together.'

'I got three...' Chastity mumbled under her breath.

'What?'

'Never mind. It's easy for them; they have the King behind them, all the spares they need, custom flightsuits, while what are we flying?'

'Spits!' Collingwood grinned. 'Bloody marvellous Supranaval Spitsteams!'

'Clapped out Mark Ones!'

'It could be worse; we could still be flying the Brummells.'

Chastity shuddered at the thought of the machines the squadron had been formed to fly. The *Brummell Aggressor* had been designed at a time when the bigwigs in the RAC, every single one of whom had fought in the First Great War, had been convinced that, if war came, then they would be defending Britain against massed formations of unescorted enemy airships. They were heavily armoured and had a turret in the middle of the fuselage, but were underpowered, heavy, and extremely slow. They had been shot down in droves in France when they had come up against the modern fighters of *Die Fliegertruppe*. Thankfully, though, 92 Squadron had been one of the first to convert to Spitsteams, just before they had been sent over the channel. Unfortunately, they were still flying those same Spitsteams, with hundreds of hours on them, whereas most other squadrons had the more recent Mark Two versions of the Spitsteam and Harridan and the Misfits were flying custom designed and hand-crafted aircraft.

'They're probably not even very good pilots, but just rich kids who've paid for their commissions.'

'Gwen Stone isn't.'

Chastity sniffed dismissively. 'Nobody knows much about her. Even if she's *not* from a rich family she'll probably end up having *some* family connection or other, like being the War Minister's niece. You mark my words.'

A fresh burst of laughter drew their attention back to the group and they looked over to see that Porter was now standing in the middle of it, speaking so loudly that his words easily carried to them.

'You know, I was almost a Misfit.'

'No!' The men around him were mesmerised by whatever story he was telling and the answer was chorused by all of them.

'I was! The Abbess came to see me one day and she said to me... you know what she said?'

'No?'

'She said: Rupert, I *want* you.'

There was crude laughter from the group and Chastity and Collingwood exchanged a distasteful look.

'I kid you not! She said: Rupert I want you.'

'And what did you say to her?'

'I said: not now love, dinner's in half an hour.'

There was more laughter and Chastity growled and pushed herself to her feet.

Collingwood looked up at her in alarm. 'What are you doing?'

'I'm going to put a stop to this.'

'I thought you didn't like the Misfits?'

'I don't, but I dislike Porter and everything he stands for even more.'

Chastity stomped over towards them, her heavy flying boots not making nearly as impressive sound on the grass as she would have liked. She came to a halt on the outside of the circle, facing Porter, who was still telling of his supposed encounter with the leader of the Misfits.

'She's screwing up that sour puss of hers and I can tell she wants me, but I'm not going to just give it up, am I?'

The laughter from the pilots was cruder than ever as Porter approached the climax of his story.

'So I...' Porter frowned and stopped when he caught sight of Chastity.

'What the hell do you want, Arrowsmith?'

Any doubts about what she intended to do disappeared completely when he sneered, his eyes going slowly up and down her body.

'I was just wondering what happened today?'

'I told you - I was having problems with my spring and had to return to base.'

'Again?'

'You know how these old springs get, *Sergeant.*'

He waved at her dismissively, pulling rank in an effort to shut her up, and turned away to resume his story, but she'd had enough and wasn't going to let him get away with his dishonesty anymore.

'That's funny, because your fitters swapped your spring out for a brand new one last night. But, then again, a new spring slips just like an old one with hundreds of hours of flight time, doesn't it, *Sir*?'

For the first time, the faces of the men around Porter showed something other than amusement and derision and there was some uncomfortable shuffling and quite a few uncertain looks shot at Porter.

The man glanced around his group of cronies and frowned when he saw their expressions. He stalked over to her and stood as close as he could, looming above her, using his six foot frame in an attempt to make her feel small and helpless. Chastity had plenty of experience dealing with bullies, though, and was very familiar with the tactics they used, so she was able to keep her expression impassive while he spoke down at her.

'Now, look here, *Chastity*. I know living up to that name of yours has you frustrated, but you don't have to take it out on me.' He put his hand on her arm and smiled down at her. 'I would be more than willing to let you take those frustrations out on me another way, though...'

Chastity looked up at him. He was certainly handsome, in that floppy-haired, public schoolboy way and his boasting probably worked on many of the women he tried to work his charm on, especially when he was in uniform. She could see through it all, though, right to his rotten core.

She smiled back at him and batted her eyelids, then brought her knee up sharply.

'I would have punched him, sir, but if I'd hurt him badly enough to ground him he would've just got what he wanted. He might be uncomfortable for a while, but he doesn't need *them* to fly.'

Chastity stood at attention in front of the base commander's desk. She was trying to stare at a point on the wall above the man's head, like she'd been taught, but her eyes kept being drawn to a smudge on the light green paint a couple of feet to the side. Someone had written something in pencil then not rubbed it out properly and the mark which had been left looked uncannily like an enemy fighter hovering several thousand feet above, waiting to pounce. It was far more disconcerting than the frown on the officer's face and she wondered if he knew that and had left it there deliberately.

'I appreciate the thoughtfulness, Aviator Sergeant, but I'm afraid it will do nothing to help your case.'

'My case, sir?' She blinked and looked at the commander for the first time. After the open belligerence she had encountered among the rest of the men of the squadron she was somewhat surprised to see sympathy and something akin to regret blossom in his expression and her best "authority confronting face" slipped slightly, although, when she thought about it, she thought she knew why.

Wing Commander Reginald Brice, like many of the old guard who filled the higher ranks of the RAC, had been a pilot during the Great War and, as such, he had flown alongside many women. It seemed he didn't share the same prejudices as the younger men. Those men had grown up in the long years of peace, during which women had been encouraged to stay at home and raise children to replace a generation who had been almost entirely lost in the trenches.

However, that didn't mean he didn't know that point of view existed.

'Even though there were,' he gave her a look full of meaning, '*extenuating circumstances* you still struck an officer and there is nothing I can do to prevent your court martial.'

'But, sir...'

Brice held up a hand to stop her. 'However, I need all the good pilots I can get right now, especially with the wastrels I've been stuck with. So, until things quiet down a bit and there's time to get together a tribunal, you are still flying, but you're confined to quarters while off duty.' He smiled wryly. 'Which is a bit of a shame, especially today of all days; the squadron has been invited to a shindig on Misfit Squadron's base.'

Chastity hid her relief at not having to go to a party thrown by the Misfits. She couldn't think of anything she'd want less than to attend something which was obviously just a bone being thrown by the "elite" squadron to the other squadrons of the RAC.

She didn't express her opinion, but instead just concentrated on the fact that she could keep flying.

'Thank you, sir.'

'I'm just doing what I can for the good of the country, Arrowsmith.' Brice sighed. 'You had a bloody good record up till now and more kills than most, outside of the Misfits. I'll do my best to put in a good word for you, but you'd better do something pretty damn spectacular over the next few days if you want the board to look favourably on you.'

'I'll give it my best shot, sir.'

'I'm sure you will.' Brice gave her a nod, then looked down at the mess of paperwork on his desk.

Chastity turned to go, but then hesitated. Continuing a conversation after being dismissed wasn't done, but she just had to know. 'And Aviator Lieutenant Porter, sir?'

Brice looked up at her, his face thunderous. 'Porter will get what's coming to him, don't you worry.'

92 Squadron were sent up twice more that day to intercept small raids heading for Folkestone and Portsmouth. After the morning's events, Chastity was extremely relieved to find that the order of battle on the blackboard in the dispersal hut had been changed and she had been placed on Roberta Collingwood's wing as number four of blue flight.

The two women were the same rank, but Collingwood had joined the RAC one month before her. Even though Charity had been moved up a class at basic training because of her military background and they had graduated at the same time, that initial month meant everything as far as seniority was concerned. So, despite the fact that they both knew that Chastity was by far the better pilot, Collingwood had to be element leader.

In the meantime, Porter had been put on the wing of Squadron Leader Sanders, the squadron commander, probably so that Sanders could keep an eye on him.

Porter had been called to Brice's office immediately after Chastity. The people working in the room outside his office had tried their hardest to listen in, but the conversation within had taken place so quietly that they had been unable to hear a word. They just reported that, when he left after more than a quarter of an hour, he was as white as a sheet. Funnily enough, after that he had no more problems with his spring.

The squadron was stood down at six and the pilots rushed off to pretty themselves up to go to the party on the Misfit base in Kent. Chastity still wasn't at all fussed about missing the party itself, but she really would have liked to get a look at their aircraft and found that she was quite upset about the missed opportunity. It was a small consolation when she found out that Porter wasn't going either - he too had been confined to the base, but whether he was up on charges or not, nobody knew, and he wasn't saying.

Collingwood saw her long face and paused in doing her makeup - as the only two women they were the only occupants in the large eight-person room in the barracks. 'Buck up, Chas, I'll smuggle you back a bottle of wine or something. I've heard they have a fully stocked cellar on their base.'

'Don't bother.' Chastity shook her head. 'I'm not much of a drinker.'

'Alright then, I'll smuggle you back one of their machines.'

Chastity huffed in amusement. 'Now, *that* I wouldn't say no to!'

The pilots hadn't gotten too much more drunk than they did on any given night, so hangovers weren't too severe the next morning when they showed up for the dawn patrol, but Porter still tried to poke fun at anyone he could, as he usually did. None of his former friends played his game, though, they just gave him the cold shoulder.

The patrol was uneventful, but when the squadron landed they were rushed straight into a briefing in Biggin's underground briefing hall.

Three squadrons were based on the airfield, 92 and 72, equipped with Spitsteams and part of 141, flying Brummells which had been converted to night fighters after their poor showing at the beginning of the war. They packed into the cold, damp, bare concrete room along with 66 Squadron - the last squadron in the Biggin Hill sector, who were based at Gravesend, but had flown in for the briefing and shivered with the contrast in temperature with the Indian summer, which was keeping the skies over England clear and allowing the British pilots so little relief.

'Ten-shun!' The NCO standing watch by the door at the side of the briefing room called the pilots to attention as Wing Commander Brice strode in.

The NCO's order was crisp and sharp, but the response most definitely wasn't, the pilots weary after a long summer of fighting and not really into the whole discipline thing anyway.

The only one who made any kind of effort was Chastity, but that was because she'd been brought up in a military family with her mother a regimental sergeant major and her father a combat medic. As a child, while her mother was walking her to the army base school, she'd once asked (a little too loudly) why she had saluted an officer half her age who was stumbling about in the early morning, drunkenly making his way back from a night out. Her mother had answered equally loudly. 'You salute the rank, not the man. He might be the most useless berk who ever lived, but for some reason he holds a commission and *that* is from the King. He is the one who has to make sure he is worthy of that.' Chastity had glanced back at the man and had seen him stop, head down. He'd taken a deep breath then straightened his back and made a supreme effort to walk in a straight line. Her mother's grunt had puzzled her at the time, but the incident had stuck in her mind and years later she had realised that the grunt had been one of satisfaction and it was just one of her mother's many ways of teaching without teaching. It was a technique she had used until the day she'd died - her parents' regiment had been part of the British Exploration Force sent to France in the early days of the war and they had both been killed in the retreat on Dunkirk, while Chastity had been fighting in the skies above them.

'Sit, please.' Brice called out as he walked down the aisle to the front of the room. He barely waited for everyone to settle down before beginning to speak. 'Right then, we're finally taking it to the Boche today. The bigwigs at Whitehall have finally realised that they really should do something about that little invasion fleet waiting over the Channel and have decided to send over the bombers.'

He nodded to an orderly, standing by at the free-standing map board and he threw back the blanket covering it to reveal a large map showing the south coast of England and the north coast of France. Red ribbons were pinned on it to show the routes that five different raids would be taking from the various air bases in southern England to five enemy-held ports, four in France and one in Belgium.

'In a couple of hours, every Nelson and Splendid we've got is being sent across to attack the five ports that show the biggest concentrations of enemy vessels - Ostend, Dunkirk, Calais, Boulogne, and Le Havre. We have been assigned to escort the raid going to Calais. 72 and 92 will be going up for top cover, while 141 and 66 will be providing close coverage.'

There were groans at that from the pilots of 66 Squadron. Close coverage meant flying in formation with the bombers, which was alright for the Brummells of 141 because they were slower and were ideal for the more static role with the heavy cannons in their turrets, but 66 Squadron's Spitsteams would suffer horribly from being tied down and be more vulnerable because of it.

Brice ignored them; it wasn't the first time the squadrons under his command had been called to do something they weren't suited to and it wouldn't be the last. He did, however, nod at Squadron Leader Sanders, who had put his hand up.

'Won't we be spread a bit thin, sir? I'm down to seven aircraft. 72 have, what, eight? Nine? Jim?'

He searched out Squadron Leader James McLeod, the commander of 72 squadron, who laughed and shook his head. 'Try five!'

'I've got nine available, maybe one more if the fitters pull off a miracle,' called out Aviator Lieutenant Tunstall, the temporary commander of 66 Squadron after the previous commander had been killed the day before.

Sanders grunted. 'So, that's twenty-one, maybe twenty-two, and the four Brummells. It's not nearly enough! The Fleas have got hundreds of fighters along that coast!'

Brice nodded. 'Normally, I would agree with you, but we are going to be reinforced by a squadron from another sector, bringing us up to something like thirty fighters.'

'How? How are they spare?' Sanders frowned. 'Five raids, thirty or forty fighters to cover each... The last reports say we don't *have* a hundred and fifty fighters to put up in the air, let alone two hundred or more, unless we commit the reserves, which would be suicide.'

Brice smiled wryly. 'We don't have to cover all five raids, though, just three of them. For some reason, it has been decided that Misfit Squadron will be covering *both* the groups heading to Ostend and Dunkirk *on their own* while everybody else takes care of the rest.'

Disbelieving silence greeted Brice's revelation and he took advantage of it to bring the briefing to a rapid conclusion.

'Ensuring the survival of the bombers is the primary mission here. If the enemy fighters break off for home you are not to pursue, you are to stay with the bombers and protect them until they are all the way home.' He glanced down at the chronograph on his wrist. 'Takeoff is in two hours at twelve fifteen hours and the rendezvous is at twenty-five thousand feet over Maidstone. Dismissed.'

The rendezvous points for four of the five raids heading across the Channel were in the skies over Kent and there were more aircraft in the sky than Chastity had seen since the flypast of Trafalgar Square she'd taken part in for Empire Day in 1938. However, she, and most of the pilots, only had eyes for a single small group of them - the multi-coloured machines of Misfit Squadron.

Despite the fact that they had been fighting over Britain for months and before that over France, just as she had, it was the first time she was actually seeing the famous aircraft. She had actually been convinced at one point at the beginning of the summer that they didn't actually exist, that they were just an invention of the British Press or Whitehall's all-powerful propaganda machine, but there they were, just ten miles away, as clear as day through her excellent RAC lenses.

There were eight of them, four large twin-springed machines and four smaller single-springed ones. Thanks to the press she knew the names of all of them and had read about the unbelievable things that they had been credited with. The identities of the pilots had been kept out of the newspapers, though, but that an ineffectual measure to say the least; the RAC grapevine had provided that information weeks ago and most of the Corps had heard within hours when a new pilot, Gwen Stone, had been chosen to join the squadron and pilot *Wasp*, which had been languishing in a hangar since the death of her pilot. With their rumoured spy network, the Prussians had more than likely found out who they were as well and the British public were probably the only ones not in the know.

She took in the lines of the eight machines. They were superb, each and every one of them not only a masterpiece of design, expertly adapted to warfare, but managing to express the individuality of their pilots at the same time.

'Lovely sight, aren't they, Blue Four?'

Chastity glanced across at Collingwood. 'The machines are lovely, yes, Blue Three, but I don't think much of their formation; it's a bit bloody sloppy.'

Collingwood laughed. 'Nothing's ever good enough for you is it, Chas?'

'Some things are... My flying, for example.' Chastity grinned as Collingwood glanced back at her and crossed her eyes.

'And what do you think of the big one with the bombers?'

'The big one?'

Chastity frowned, she had been so absorbed with the small fighters that she hadn't even seen *Dreadnought*, the Misfit gun platform, which the RAC rumour machine had placed on the mission.

It wasn't hard to spot.

'Bloody hell, what is that paint job?'

'Dazzle camouflage.'

'I know that!' Chastity rolled her eyes. 'It was a rhetorical question. What I really meant was - what kind of psychopath would paint their machine like that?'

The machine was a massive six-engined beast, which easily dwarfed the four-engined Splendids and twin-engined Nelsons it was holding formation with. It was also eye-achingly painted in a camouflage pattern which had originally been used on ships in the First Great War - intended to confuse the enemy and make it difficult for them to estimate the range to a ship, its speed, or even which way it was moving. She had to admit, despite how awful it looked, it was actually quite effective on the aircraft. It was almost as big as a ship anyway.

'All Charlie aircraft, come to heading one one oh, sixty miles to target.' Chastity put the Misfits out of her mind as the leader of the bomber formation going to Calais, codenamed "Charlie" for the raid, called his charges to order. She followed the rest of the Spitsteams as they turned onto the heading and powered out over the Channel, forging ahead to intercept any enemy fighters that appeared, before they got to the bombers.

Chastity threw her helmet onto her bed and shoved the palms of her hands into her eyes, desperately fighting to not break down into tears. She lost and her legs gave out beneath her, sending her crumpling to the floor.

She didn't know who had screamed out the warning, but it had come far too late.

More than 70 Prussian fighters had been waiting for them twenty miles from the coast, loitering out of sight, high in the sky at their service ceiling, and the Spitsteams flying top cover hadn't been able to react in time when they swooped, guns blazing.

Seven of the twelve British fighters were destroyed immediately, among them, she found out later, those of Sanders and Porter. However, by the time the survivors turned to fight, they found that the enemy had just passed them by and were already diving on the bomber formation.

The Spitsteams in close support had more warning and were able to accelerate towards the threat, but the Fleas just ignored them and went after the larger aircraft and the Brummells. All four of the Brummells fell in just that first pass, as did three of the Scott Splendids, which the Calais raid was composed of. Half a dozen more dropped out of the formation, unable to maintain their height or keep up, and began a long turn for home.

Chastity had broken away from Collingwood during the attack, making it harder for them to be targeted, but she fell back in onto her wing as they dived after the Prussians.

Collingwood glanced across at her and grinned. 'Any damage, Blue Four?'

'None, Three, you?'

'I've got a couple of lovely holes in my right wing, but that's it.'

'Nothing stopping us getting our own back, then, is there Berty?'

'Nothing, Chas. Let's see how many you can get today!'

In not coming back around to finish off the Spitsteams the Fleas had handed the height advantage to the RAC, and the remaining fighters were able to pay them back in kind. However, with far fewer machines, their attack was far less effective and only two of the Prussian fighters were forced away, one of which was able to limp back in the direction of the French coast. The advantage had been spent, though, and the two groups of Spitsteams joined up to try to repel the marauders.

The fighter squadrons of the RAC had been outnumbered in the skies above England all summer, so it was a situation they were used to, and they were able to take down another eight enemy fighters, two of them by Chastity, for only one more loss. However, the Prussians didn't seem to care; they remained single-minded in their persecution of the bombers and one after another of the Splendids were knocked from the sky.

In the end, only five of the bombers were able to drop their loads on the French port.

The Prussians broke off immediately after the bombers turned for home, letting them go as if they didn't care about them, and Squadron Leader McLeod, in command of the fighters, ordered the Spitsteams not to follow.

It had been a very small and very dejected group of fighters who returned to Biggin Hill, but the final victim of the raid hadn't yet been claimed.

Collingwood's right wheel strut, damaged in the initial attack without her knowledge, had given way on landing and her wing had dug into the ground at almost a hundred miles an hour. The Spitsteam had rolled over and over, tearing itself apart.

Chastity looked over at the bed next to hers through tear-filled eyes. Most pilots carried a few personal items with them wherever they went, to remind them of home, or family, or a sweetheart, and Roberta had more than most. Outside of the squadron, where she'd been forced to be professional and cool towards the male pilots so as to be respected, she had been an extrovert, who had brightened every room she'd ever been in. She had been well-liked by both sexes and had picked up admirers, mostly male, but not exclusively, wherever she went, all of whom had seemed to want to outdo the last with the lavishness of their gifts: the white silk nightshirt draped over the metal headboard was the gift of a French pilot from when 92 Squadron had been over in France; a Navy officer she'd met at a dance hall when they'd been on leave in London had given her the carved wooden model of *Dragonfly* that stood on the bedside table; the elegant woven copper and gold wire carriage clock next to it had come from royalty, or so she claimed. There were many more keepsakes like them, tucked inside a box in the storage room, and one of their favourite ways of passing the time during the long hours between flights had been to discuss the various merits or otherwise of the men who had become besotted with her, trying to pick which of her suiters she should accept.

Her company had been the only thing that had made life in the squadron, surrounded by bigots and with a coward on her wing, bearable.

And now she was gone.

Eight replacement pilots arrived at dawn the next morning, bleary eyed with the early hour but looking ever so keen. They were fresh out of flight training school and everything about them, from their impeccable uniforms, to their new kitbags, to their unwrinkled flight gear just shouted *inexperienced.* They went in to see Brice, who assigned four each to 92 and 72 Squadrons, then sent them out to their respective dispersal huts.

For some reason, the Prussians seemed to be having a bit of a lie in that morning, so Brice told the squadron commanders to get the new pilots up in the air and run them through their paces. There were two young women among the four pilots assigned to 92 - Helen Steward and Jane Easton - and Chastity wasn't at all surprised when she was perfunctorily introduced to them by Aviator Lieutenant Jones, in temporary command of the drastically reduced squadron, then ordered out of her comfy deckchair and told to take them up.

As they walked over to the line of Spitsteams, the two pilots only had eyes for the aircraft, looking to see which one was "theirs". Chastity, though, only had eyes for them.

They were desperately fresh-faced and didn't look like they were old enough to be out of school, let alone on the point of going up to take on the might of the Fliegertruppe - one of them even had freckles for heaven's sake!

She shared a look with Tom Dawkins, the Aviator Sergeant in charge of the ground crew, then nodded in the direction of the aircraft, many of which were brand new, having been ferried in overnight from the factories. 'This is Easton and Steward, Tom, which ones do you have for them?'

The grizzled veteran of the First Great War looked the two new pilots up and down and sniffed, then turned to point at the two Spitsteams next to hers with a hand covered with burn scars. 'Easton's got Nightingale and Steward's got Gladstone.' He looked back at the women and all but growled at them. 'Don't you dare put even a single scratch on my birds!' He scowled at them and when they looked away, frightened, he winked at Chastity and mouthed *good luck*, before stalking away to organise the crews getting the Spitsteams ready.

As soon as Dawkins had gone, the two pilots grinned and hurried towards their aircraft.

'Oi! Did I tell you you could go to your machines? Get your arses back here!' Chastity called them back and was dismayed when the two meekly obeyed her as if they were children, despite them both having gone through Officer Orientation College and outranking her.

They stood in front of her, waiting expectantly, barely able to stay still with the desire to jump into their Spitsteams and get into the air. She understood how they felt; once upon a time she had been exactly like them, but those days were long gone, left behind in the years between the wars, when going up in an aircraft didn't mean risking a meeting with a Flea, followed quickly by a handshake from the Dark Scythesman.

She looked at Easton. She was the youngest looking of the two, a thin waif who looked more like she was twelve than the eighteen or nineteen that she had to be. 'How many hours in Spits?'

'Ten, ma'am.'

'Don't call me, ma'am, please, *ma'am*; I have to work for a living.' She turned to Steward, who she could only describe as an English Rose and who would be eaten alive by the male pilots if they got the chance. 'You?'

'Eight, ma...uh..., Sergeant.'

Chastity grimaced. With so few hours under their belts on Spits they wouldn't know how hard they could push their machine before it broke, nor would they know any of the tricks which would help them survive when they had an MU9 on their tail. But at least they wouldn't crash on landing. 'Well, this morning we're going to add at least one to that. We're going to run through some basic aerobatics first, then you'll try to follow me as I take you through some more complicated stuff. If that goes well, then we'll finish with a few mock dogfights. Got that?'

The two pilots nodded, grinning, still far too eager for her liking.

'Any questions?'

'How many kills do you have?'

'Have you met the Misfits?'

The two girls spoke at once and she looked back and forth from one to the other, then sighed. 'Oh, just shut up and get in your aircraft.' Chastity turned away and stalked towards her own machine, Victoria. She caught Dawkins looking at her and rolled his eyes at him, but he just shook his head sadly and turned back to his work.

She knew exactly what he was thinking - new pilots like these lasted an average of two minutes in the skies of Britain.

Thankfully, the radar screens stayed empty and Chastity was able to have an uneventful flight with the two newcomers. She was able to teach them a few of the tricks that she'd learnt and was satisfied that she had done her best to prepare them for combat as best she could in the little time given her. As the day wore on, the only incidents, in fact, were a couple of raids on the south coast and a single reconnaissance aircraft, all of which were taken care of by other squadrons.

The one thing that did happened was that the report on the previous day's raids came in. Incredibly, unbelievably even, while the three raids the normal RAC squadrons had escorted had failed to do any meaningful damage, the two bomber groups shepherded by the Misfits had destroyed hundreds of invasion barges, while the Misfits themselves had shot down in the region of forty aircraft.

While most of the squadron ate up the news and downed many a drink to the Misfits in the mess that evening, Charity immediately dismissed it as more propaganda; there couldn't be such a disparity between the raids carried out by the Misfits and the rest of the RAC, it was impossible.

Perhaps that was why they had been the only escorts for the two raids; most of the bomber crews would have been too busy just trying to survive to witness the actual results of their efforts.

The next day dawned much the same as the previous one, with nothing on radar, and Chastity considered asking whether she could take Steward and Easton up again. Something told her not to, though, and at just after eleven her gut feeling was proven right as both Spitsteam squadrons at Biggin Hill were given the order to scramble.

Thanks to the reinforcements and a few pilots coming back from a couple of days of much needed rest, the two squadrons were able to put just over twenty aircraft in the air.

As soon as they were up, the voice of the controller at Biggin filled their ears over the general frequency. 'Tennis and Gannic Squadrons, this is Sapper. Incoming enemy raid, estimated two hundred and fifty plus aircraft. Heading one zero zero and make angels twenty-five, over.'

'Gannic Squadron, this is Red One. You heard the man, coming around left now.'

Lieutenant Jones' call over the squadron frequency was not part of the normal protocol for such a simple manoeuvre and Chastity frowned; he was afraid that the new pilots wouldn't react to him just turning and there would be collisions, but there were other ways of making sure there were no mishaps than as good as announcing that he had no confidence in them, like simply turning slower.

Chastity still kept an eye on Steward and Easton, on either side of her as yellow flight, as she turned onto the new heading; just because she disagreed with how he'd done it, didn't mean she didn't share his trepidation. Jones had left her with both of the girls, rather than split them up and put one each on the wing of someone experienced, like he'd done with the two male newbies, and as far as Chastity was concerned that was just more evidence of the prejudices that were rife in the squadron and the RAC in general.

She forced her frustrations out of her mind as best she could to concentrate on the job at hand; she was going to be hard enough pressed to get through the fight herself, let alone try to get her two charges through it and didn't need the distraction.

Even though she'd said everything she'd needed to say on the ground already, she switched to yellow flight's comm channel to say it again; her voice and the simple act of running through what she expected of them would focus their thoughts and stop them from thinking about how many ways they could die in the next half an hour. Her words died in her throat when she saw the enemy raid, though.

She'd heard Sapper call out the number of incoming aircraft but not really processed it until now. Two hundred and fifty aircraft comprised by far the largest single raid that had ever come across the Channel and it was already well over England, an endless line of enemy fighters and bombers, which, she saw, would only narrowly miss Biggin because it was heading straight for London.

'Say again, Yellow One?'

'What? Oh, nothing, Three.' Chastity had no idea what she'd muttered under her breath, but it was probably something she'd learned from her mother and wouldn't bear repeating.

The Biggin Spitsteams were climbing as hard as they could, but Chastity could already see that they wouldn't reach the raid before they were over London. Some fighters already had, though, and smoke trails showed where some of the large Prussian machines had already fallen, burning. She slotted lenses in place over her goggles to try to make out who they were and what was happening, but they were much too far away still.

'Gannic Leader to Sapper. Come in please.'

'Sapper here, Gannic Leader. Go ahead.'

'We're not going to get to these blighters before they've unloaded. Why the hell didn't you send us up earlier? Over.'

There were a few seconds of silence as the controller at Biggin Hill, probably in shock at Jones' bad manners and blatant breach of radio protocol, tried to decide what to say.

'Raid initially presented as one hundred plus aircraft, Gannic Leader. You were scrambled as soon as revised estimates came in.'

'That's not bloody good enough, Sapper!'

'Understood, Gannic Leader. Try to do your best even so, there's a good chap.'

There was a chiding note to the Biggin controller's dry reply that made Chastity grin widely and she suspected that Jones' hopes of being promoted and confirmed as commander of 92 Squadron hadn't been helped by the short exchange. He hadn't demonstrated anything in the way of leadership since he took over, so she wouldn't be sorry if he didn't get the squadron.

He did himself no favours with his next order, either.

'Bugger this for a lark, I want some height before I take on these blighters. Gannic Flight will turn to one four zero on my mark. Mark.'

Chastity made the course correction with the other two flights, but inside she was seething; it would mean not intercepting the raid as it got to London, but rather coming up behind it and catching it after it had turned for home. If 92 were on their own that would make sound tactical sense, especially with the new pilots, because it would allow them to confront them without a height disadvantage, but they weren't on their own and the delay in reinforcing the rest of the RAC aircraft would only cost the lives of British pilots. It was the wrong move and it was typical of someone who had been one of Porter's closest friends.

Thankfully, Biggin were listening in to the squadron comms and were almost as quick as Chastity to condemn Jones' action.

'Gannic Leader, Sapper here. Raid is on bearing zero nine zero, suggest you turn to intercept, over.'

The controller's words and tone of voice might have been placid, but there was an implied threat in them that was chilling; if Jones disobeyed the "suggestion" a court martial would be sure to follow with at least a charge of disobeying an order, but possibly one of cowardice in the face of the enemy. Not to mention that he would be ostracised by most of the country if his refusal to defend London were made public. It went without saying, though, that, whatever he did in the next few seconds, whether he came to his senses and did what everybody knew was the right thing or not, his aspirations had gone down in flames.

This time he made no announcement of his intention to turn, but everyone was expecting the move and there were no accidents.

The first of the bombers had long ago dropped their loads and turned for home when 92 Squadron finally reached twenty-five thousand feet and they were the ones that Jones led them to attack. He made no more radio calls, but just angled his flight to intercept the lead bombers. Chastity sniffed at him in disdain and continued climbing with Easton and Steward while she surveyed the enemy formation, looking for a target. The bombers had spread out a bit after turning and she soon spotted a group of forty or fifty HO111's, slightly separated from the rest, apparently without a fighter escort.

'Alright, girls, stick close, like three cogs in the same machine. Pick your targets, don't waste ammo, and for Victoria's sake don't collide with anything.'

'Roger, Leader.'

'Roger.'

Chastity took them in and began making fast sweeping runs at the bombers, each one at a sight angle so as to reduce the very real possibility of collision she'd mentioned. She didn't press her Spitsteam quite as hard as she usually did, so as to give her wingmates a chance to keep up with her, and was pleasantly surprised when they not only did, but also managed to get in a few solid shots of their own.

It was almost easy, the Spitsteams moving at such speed that the return fire from the bombers seemed unable to touch them, and four of the large machines dropped from the sky with catastrophic damage.

It couldn't last, though, and everything changed when the escort arrived.

Chastity saw them first - a flight of MU9's racing to the aid of their slower comrades. They were already too close to avoid or climb above, so there were only a few choices of what to do and she ran through the options in an instant.

Easton and Sanders had acquitted themselves well, much better than she'd expected, but they weren't ready to face the experienced fighter pilots, so fighting was out of the question. As was just turning and running; that would be abandoning the other RAC pilots and make her as no better than Jones. The last option, then, was the only one and it was also the best as far as she and the war in the sky were concerned.

'Heads up, girls, we've got enemy fighters at ten o'clock. We're going to ignore them for now, though, and do a couple more passes on the one-elevens before getting the hell out and back to Biggin, understood?'

There was a nervous hesitation to the two women's acknowledgements when they came that was completely understandable, but there was no time to reassure them as Chastity dived back into the bomber formation, closely followed by the MU's. She pushed her Spitsteam much harder than before, trusting that fear and adrenaline would spur on her wingmates and help them to keep up with her. She spun around and over bombers, pulled maximum rate turns behind them and squeezing off shot after shot, always with an eye to the enemy fighters, making sure that there was always at least one of the large machines between her flight and them.

She kept going as long as she dared, but the Prussians were getting closer and her wingmates were looking ragged, their formation getting more and more loose with each parting second and their shots, when they came, going wider and wider. She herself was also running low on ammunition, so she decided it was time to call it a day.

'Yellow flight, on my mark, invert and dive.'

Chastity headed straight for the largest clump of bombers. She opened fire at extreme range and was pleased to see tracers racing past her on either side as her wingmates followed suit. She kept her finger on the button as she danced on her rudder pedals, weaving back and forth, sowing as much chaos as she could, until her guns clicked on empty. She wasn't finished there, though, and she aimed her nose straight at the leader. She held the collision course until she could see the panicked face of the pilot and pulled up at the last second, passing over the huge tail of the bomber with only feet to spare as the machine dived away, belatedly trying to avoid a collision that was never going to come.

'Mark!'

She shouted into the comms, waited a heartbeat, then rolled her Spitsteam onto its back and pulled the stick into her lap, sending her aircraft flashing between two more of the enemy machines.

The G forces piled on and she screamed to keep the blood from rushing out of her brain and rendering her unconscious. The pressure soon came off though as she eased the stick back to neutral to let the Spitsteam fall almost vertically and she spared the time to glance to either side, where Easton and Sanders should be. Her stomach churned when she found only found Easton and she clicked on her radio as she craned her neck to look behind, hoping that Sanders had just been forced to roll to the other side or something. 'Yellow Three, where are you?'

There was no reply, though, and she sighed, but then put the girl out of her mind; she still had to get herself and Easton home safely. Puzzlingly, though, when she searched for pursuers she found none; the fighters had stayed with the bombers.

A quick glance at the familiar scenery below told her where she was and she pulled out of the dive slightly and headed directly for Biggin.

'Hang on a tick, would you, Arrowsmith? I want a word.'

Chastity looked back at Barbara Yarrow in surprise. She and Easton had just made their reports and had already gotten up to go when the intelligence officer had called her back.

'Yes, ma'am.' Chastity turned to Easton. 'Go ahead, I'll catch up.'

The thin waif nodded and smiled, but her complexion, even whiter than usual, and the twitch at the corner of her mouth betrayed how much having to go up to face so many enemy aircraft on her first ever combat sortie had affected her.

She watched the girl go on unsteady legs, and only when she had stepped out into the sunshine did she turn back to Yarrow.

'It's Sanders isn't it?' she asked quietly.

Yarrow nodded. 'I didn't want to say anything in front of Easton.' She glanced down at her notes. 'Her Spitsteam went down just outside of Sidcup with her still inside.'

'I thought... I'd hoped she...' Chastity sighed. 'Never mind.'

'I'm sorry, but didn't think I should be the one to tell Easton.'

'You're right, it should be me. Thank you, ma'am. I'll do it tonight, after flying.' She nodded then turned to go, leaving unsaid what they both mentally added in their minds anyway - *if she survives*.

She turned back after only a couple of steps, though. 'You know, I don't think I hit that share actually.'

Chastity had bagged two bombers outright and had shared one each with her pilots. Renouncing her claim on one of the shares would give it entirely to Sanders. It was an empty gesture which would do nothing to bring the girl back, but it might go some way to consoling her parents, knowing that their daughter had done her damnedest and taken some of the enemy with her.

Yarrow nodded and made a note. 'Good show, Arrowsmith.'

Chastity hurried over to the NAACI van and took her meal from the volunteer - potatoes and cabbage *again*, with a sorry looking carrot and tinned meat - then went to find Easton. The girl was sitting on the floor, on her own away from the few other survivors of the morning's flight, leaning against the side of the dispersal hut with her plate in her lap and a tin cup of water on the grass next to her.

Chastity sat down next to her and began eating, stuffing the unappetising food into her mouth and swallowing it as quickly as she could, not because she was hungry, but so as not to taste it as much. Thankfully, though, rations were a bit short at the moment and there wasn't much of it to eat. The girl was only picking at her food and she nudged her. 'You've got to eat. If you don't you might pass out in the cockpit; pure oxygen and hunger don't mix well, believe me.'

It was a lie, but the poor quality of the food would give her something else to think about, aside from her own mortality. She also looked as undernourished as a Dickens orphan.

'You know, you did quite well...' Chastity began.

'Arrowsmith!' The bellow came from the door of the dispersal hut, only a few yards away, cutting her off. Apparently, the duty NCO hadn't seen her around the corner and had taken his annoyance out on the eardrums of everyone within fifty yards.

'Here!' Chastity called out, leaning forwards and waving at the man.

He turned and scowled at her. 'Squadron Leader Brice wants you. Sharpish!'

'Thank you, Corporal.'

Chastity groaned and got to her feet. She contemplated taking her food with her, but rejected the idea; she didn't think she'd be able to keep the food down on the bumpy ride to the main buildings. Throwing it away was out of the question, though, so she held the plate out to Easton. 'Here, get this down you as well.'

The girl took it, but Chastity didn't wait to see if she ate it or not, she just jogged over to the open-topped autocar that was always standing by to ferry the staff around.

Brice was in his office, pacing up and down while he shouted into a radio receiver as his secretary cringed beside the wall, frantically making notes, trying to keep up with his rant. He broke off as soon as Chastity appeared in the open doorway, though, telling whoever was on the other end that he would call them back.

'Come in, Arrowsmith!' He jerked his thumb at the receiver. 'That new War Minister is a real berk, isn't he?'

'I wouldn't know, sir.'

'Trust me, he is.' Brice stalked over to his desk and sat down. He looked up at her and took a deep breath to calm his nerves. 'Well, there's no good way to say this, so here goes. We've just got confirmation that Jones bought it this morning. That leaves 92 with just new recruits and three sergeant pilots - you Thomson and Anderson and you're senior. So, until we get another squadron commander posted, which will probably be tomorrow, maybe the day after, you've got the squadron.'

Chastity opened her mouth to protest, but he just shook his head. 'That's final, Arrowsmith and I'm sure you'll do fine. Oh, and two more pilots arrived while you were up, so you're back up to eight.'

'Do I have some time to take them up, sir?'

'I don't see why...'

Brice broke off when the radio squawked and he watched as his secretary picked up the receiver.

'Commander's office.' The man listened briefly then put the receiver back and looked at Brice. '92 and 72 to five minute readiness, sir.'

Brice shrugged at Chastity. 'Sorry, Arrowsmith, looks like they're going to have to take their chances without your tutelage. Good luck.'

'Thank you, sir.'

Chastity barely waited until she was out of the door before breaking into a run.

She arrived back at dispersal just as the scramble order came in and leapt out of the autocar and straight into her Spitsteam. She shrugged into her glidewings and life vest and did up her straps as she was taxiing to the end of the airstrip, then, as soon as everyone was in the air and on the heading Sapper had given them, putting the black smoke of a still-burning London behind them, she called out the order of battle and formed her aircraft up. As squadron commander, she took the lead as Red One and assigned Thomson to lead Blue flight, leaving him to sort out his own pilots. She put one of the new pilots, whose names she didn't know, on her wing and told Easton to take the second element with the second new pilot on her wing - Easton's single combat mission wasn't much experience, but it was more than the other two had.

The incoming enemy raid was even bigger than the previous massive one, numbering an unbelievable and extremely daunting four hundred and fifty aircraft and the British had thrown everything they had into the air to respond. The Biggin squadrons found more than a hundred aircraft already aloft in the skies over Kent, cruising towards the enemy, including not only the Misfits, but the Royal Guard Squadron as well.

It was impressive, with more British fighters in the skies at the same time than there had been since the start of the war, but Chastity couldn't help but wonder just how many were being flown by men and women with little or no experience, like her own pilots. She was also more than a little concerned about the fact that, if the elite Royal Guard, the last bastion of defence for the Royal Family, had been committed to the fight, then Whitehall was likely expecting this to be Britain's last stand and, if the day's battle was lost, then the RAC would have very little left to stop the invasion fleet they'd failed to destroy only two days before.

Chastity had only just led her aircraft into formation with another couple of Spitsteam squadrons when the radio crackled and someone cleared their throat in her ears. She frowned, wondering who would possibly have such poor radio discipline and yet be transmitting on the general frequency - she hoped nothing had happened to the usual controller; they couldn't afford any chaos that day of all days.

It wasn't a controller who came on, though, but she still recognised the voice and unconsciously sat up straighter in her seat as the King began to speak in his familiar, hesitant fashion.

'Hello, brave pilots of the RAC. I am speaking to you from the eleven group control room at Uxbridge, where I will remain throughout this fateful day so that I can be as close to you as possible during this most difficult of times.'

The King paused and Chastity could almost hear him preparing himself to continue; he had famously fought with a speech impediment since a very early age and still had difficulty speaking in public.

'I could easily make a long-winded speech saying that England expects every man and woman to do his duty, or that this will be your finest hour, but I won't; I will save those platitudes for the people and for after the day's work is done because you already know what is at stake and you are well equipped to face the threat that is coming. What I will say, though, is that the thoughts and the hopes of an entire nation are with you. Take our strength, make it your own and come home victorious. Good speed and happy hunting. Out.'

There were a few moments of silence after the King finished his speech, but then Sapper came on, speaking urgently. Chastity found it hard to follow his orders; she was so used to the national anthem being played after the King spoke on the wireless that she had been taken by surprise when it hadn't, but she quickly got the gist of what he was saying.

Apparently, the raid had split up to form three columns. About a hundred fighters, including Gannic Squadron and Badger Squadron - the Misfits - were detailed to intercept the biggest one, which was arriving first, while the rest of the fighters, including the few squadrons that were still climbing hard to join them, were assigned to the other two.

Chastity turned onto the new heading that Sapper provided and accelerated with the rest of the British aircraft, more determined than ever to do her utmost to head off the bombers before they reached their apparent destination - London.

A flash of sunlight off a canopy caught her attention and she glanced to her left in time to see the colourful aircraft of Misfit Squadron climbing away at an astonishing rate, which the Spitsteams couldn't hope to match, but still staying level with the rest of the fighters.

'Those are some machines...'

Chastity scowled. 'Maintain radio discipline, please, Red Three.'

'Sorry, Leader.'

She was thinking the same thing as Easton, even as she told her off, though, and she smiled sadly as she remembered Collingwood joking about stealing one of the aircraft for her. She could have done with one of them just about then and probably would have handled it better than most of the pilots whose hands they were in.

She put such thoughts out of her mind quickly; she already had too many doubts about her wingmate and the rest of her flight and didn't want to go into battle doubting the Misfits as well. Speaking of which...

'Red Two, what's your name?'

'Excuse me, Leader?'

'Your name. I didn't get a chance to find out on the ground.'

'Fletcher, ma'am, Johnny Fletcher.'

Chastity laughed. 'That's a good sign.'

'Ma'am?'

'My surname's Arrowsmith.'

'Ah!'

The young man on her wing chuckled, which was also a good sign; it meant that he wasn't as nervous as she'd feared. She glanced at him and found him smiling in her direction. She returned his smile, but quickly turned away again; he had piercing blue eyes and wisps of curly blonde hair poking out from under his helmet and looked even younger than Easton and she hated to think how quickly he had been rushed into combat "readiness".

'Stick to me like glue, Two. Feel free to take shots at whatever you can, but don't get distracted and don't stray. Understood?'

'Roger, Leader.'

The enemy raid came inexorably closer, the aircraft appeared to cover the entire sky - more than a hundred and fifty aircraft, bobbing up and down in the air currents, the fighters criss-crossing through and over the more stately bombers. Chastity could make out the individual enemy machines now and she tried to see if there were any unescorted bombers she could single out as she had that morning. There were none, though; attacking a raid which still held its formation was a much different prospect than attacking one which had already carried out its run and been broken apart by enemy action. She angled 92 squadron towards one of the flanks of the raid anyway, thinking that her pilots would have a better chance if she could keep them on the outskirts of the fight and have the threat coming from only one side.

Chastity took a deep breath and wriggled in her seat, making sure she was comfortable, then gave each of her straps a tug and scanned her instruments one last time. As she flipped off the safety catch on her weapons she had a thought. 'Safety catches off, please, Gannic Squadron.'

She sighed when there were a couple of sheepish acknowledgements; it wasn't as if the pilots wouldn't notice as soon as they tried to fire, but it would distract them for a couple of seconds, which might well mean their deaths.

'For what we are about to receive...'

It was Easton's voice again, but this time she used the general channel for her irreverent breach of radio discipline instead of just the flight one. Chastity didn't pull her up on it, though, and neither did anyone else; they were all too fixed on the incoming machines.

After the long approach, during which the two forces had seemed to creep towards each other, it felt like the last few miles were closed in a rush. Chastity fixed on the target she'd chosen as it loomed large in her windscreen - the lead bomber of a large flight - and opened fire at extreme range, trusting in her steady hand and the British workmanship of the Whiting machine guns and Anglo Helvetia cannon to send the bullets exactly where she wanted them. The bulbous glass cockpit of the HO111 disintegrated, as did the bodies of the men within it, but she barely noticed because she was already moving on to her next victim.

Chastity usually lost herself when she was fighting. She became so focussed on what she was doing - her eyes darting this way and that, her mind calculating trajectories, her hands and feet obeying orders that were barely given - that there was barely any room for anything else. She became one with her aircraft almost, became *like* it even; emotionless and cold, with only one purpose - vanquishing the enemy.

For some reason this fight was different, though. Whether it was the squadron in her care, or because the stakes were so high, she found she just couldn't achieve that extreme level of concentration where the world beyond her immediate influence faded to nothing, and things leaked in to distract her.

She saw Blue Four disappear in a cloud of steam, fire, and black smoke as he failed to pull up in time and collided with an HO111.

She saw the Misfits appear out of nowhere and blast a gigantic hole through the middle of the bomber formation, sending the enemy into a panic which completely destroyed any cohesion they might still have, perfectly carrying out a manoeuvre that would have caused most pilots to crash, or at least clip something on their way past.

She saw the engine of an FU88 explode, sending the out of control machine careening into another. The tangled mess spun over and over as it fell out of the sky, so wildly that she doubted any of the crew would be able to get out.

She watched, amazed, as the Misfit aircraft, Wasp, chopped a bomber in two by jettisoning a spare spring at it.

She heard Easton scream in agony, before being suddenly cut off.

She saw new fires bloom in a city which was already burning.

She didn't notice when she lost Fletcher.

She did however see two of the Misfit aircraft get shot down and each time she spared a brief moment to hope that the pilots were alright; she had seen enough of the way they flew and fought in just that one battle to know that her feelings towards them had been unjustified. She now knew their worth, knew that the stories about them hadn't been exaggerated. More than anything, though, she knew that the British would need them if they were to survive the war.

When she finally ran out of ammunition she merely told whoever was still alive that she was breaking off and flew back to Biggin.

She said nothing to her fitters, who immediately began rearming and rewinding her aircraft, but just went and sat against the side wall of the dispersal hut and stared at the sky, where smoke and vapour trails still lingered.

Everything had been done that could have been done, nothing had been held back, she was sure of that. Desperately young men and women, who had no right to have been in combat, who should have been starting at university, or learning a craft, or beginning a career, had fought valiantly and many of them, too many, had died. And those experienced pilots like her had done what they had done every day over the long, hot, clear-skied summer - they had unflinchingly gone up to face overwhelming odds, knowing that their survival, the survival of the kingdom, and perhaps the survival of freedom itself, depended on them.

They had done their best. Each and every one of them. She didn't know whether it would be good enough in the end, whether it would be enough to save Britain from the vast forces that were arrayed against them, but it didn't really matter; the pilots, all of them, would keep fighting no matter what.

She took a deep breath and dropped her eyes to look through the perimeter fence at the houses of the nearby village. Many of those homes had been hit by bombs when the Fleas had been plastering Biggin, but when they had turned their ire on London the villagers had rebuilt and come back stronger and more determined.

The RAC would do the same if given half the chance.

She smiled. She had gone around the side of the hut to be alone, but there was no need; there were no tears for her to hide. Not today.

She struggled wearily to her feet and made her way into the hut to give her report to Yarrow - it would be a while before her aircraft would be ready for her to go back up and she thought she might as well use the time constructively.

THE HUNTERS

THE HUNTERS

St Petersburg, Muscovy, October 1940

Tanya leaned back in her seat and sighed in contentment. She eyed the last remaining *pelmeni* in the dish in the centre of the table, but decided not to help herself; she could always eat something at the Military Club later. Instead, she nudged them towards her younger sister, Galina. With rationing as tight as it was, the seven-year-old was looking very thin and could do with an extra helping.

She smiled as Galina's eyes lit up and grabbed the dish with two hands, but the girl had the presence of mind, despite her hunger, to glance around the table at the others before taking them. Seeing only smiles from her mother and paternal grandparents she tipped the dish, spilling the four remaining dumplings onto her plate. A healthy dollop of sour cream followed them and they disappeared one after another in rapid succession into the girl's mouth. Her grin was more than enough payment for the sacrifice.

'So, what do you have planned for your last day of leave, Tatiana?' Tanya's mother asked.

'I was going to go to the Club, I...'

'Will you take me to the ballet?' Galina blurted out.

Tanya stared at her sister, momentarily lost for words. Galina had never ever expressed an interest in the ballet, not in watching it and certainly not in doing it. 'I thought you didn't like it?'

'I don't, but the Misfits are going to be there and I want them to sign my book!'

Galina pulled a small book from the deep pockets of her skirts and put it on the table. It was one of the mass-produced picture books, with cheap cardboard pages, which were printed with colourful depictions of aircraft, in this case the British *Misfit Squadron* aircraft. It was tatty and worn from constantly being pawed at by grubby young hands.

Tanya smiled wryly. 'You know, there are some excellent Muscovite squadrons as well, like the *Black Bears*, or the *Wolfpack*. I could try to get their autographs if you want.'

Galina shook her head vigorously. 'They're not nearly as good! The Misfits are the best and bravest pilots in the world, with the best aircraft, and they're only going to be here one day. I can *always* get Muscovite autographs, but I won't get another chance to get theirs!'

Tanya pretended to think about it. 'Well, I did *really* want to go to the Club...'

'*Please?*' Galina looked at her pleadingly. She knew that Tanya was her only chance; her grandparents were taking her mother to the ministry of provisions that afternoon, to fill out the paperwork for her and Galina's food allowance to be transferred from Moscow, and they didn't have time.

'I'm not sure...' Tanya pretended to think about it, but she couldn't bring herself to tease the girl too much; there was too little happiness in her life at the moment, with her father in the army and her big sister in the air service, and she needed every little bit of it she could get. 'Oh, alright then.'

Galina squealed in delight and leapt out of her seat to wrap her arms around Tanya's neck. 'Thank you! You're the best sister ever!'

When the girl pulled back, Tanya smiled at her. 'But we're only going for a few autographs, alright? We're not going to kidnap any of them. At least not this time.'

The girl giggled, then pushed her chair back and stood. She looked at Tanya expectantly.

Tanya blinked at her in surprise. 'Now? Isn't the ballet in the evening?'

'No! They're putting on a special afternoon performance just for the Misfits! We have to hurry or we'll miss them!'

'A matinée at the Mariinsky?' Tanya's grandfather asked, incredulously. 'They never do matinées! Are you sure? Galina?'

'Of course I'm sure, dedushka! Look!' She grabbed the day's newspaper from the wooden sideboard and thrust it at the group around the dinner table - on the front page was an article covering Misfit Squadron's arrival in Muscovy. There had been articles about the British squadron most days since it had been announced they were coming to relieve the beleaguered forces on the northern front a couple of months ago and the elder members of the family had only really glanced at that day's article in passing before going on to stories that were more relevant or interesting. Galina, of course, had devoured the article and found the announcement of their visit to the ballet at the end.

Tanya's grandfather held up his hands in surrender with a smile. 'Alright! I suppose hundreds of years of tradition can be put aside for these Misfits of yours. There is a war on, after all.'

'When isn't there a war on?' Tanya's grandmother muttered under her breath.

Tanya stood and straightened her dark grey uniform, choosing to ignore the old woman. Her father's mother had lost two brothers, a sister, and a son to war and complained whenever she could, which was understandable, but it wasn't something Galina needed to be reminded of when two members of her family would be fighting soon. She made her way around the table in the cramped room, which served both as living and dining areas, and got her grey overcoat and fur-lined uniform cap from the hook next to the door. She waited while her sister packed a small bag full of pens and pencil, enough for the whole of the British Aviator Corps to sign her book at the same time, then helped her into her coat, grimacing at how thin and threadbare it was.

'Are you going to be warm enough, Galichka?'

The girl nodded enthusiastically, but didn't reply because she was already running out of the door.

Tanya shook her head and followed. She turned to smile at the adults from the doorway. 'We'll be back soon, don't eat all the *blini*!'

Grandpa's flat was about a forty minute walk from the theatre, but Galina skipped excitedly the whole way and the sisters made it in half an hour. They couldn't get anywhere near the green and white building, though, because they found the square in front of it packed with people, all equally eager as the girl to catch a glimpse of the famous pilots.

Tanya stood on the margins, looking for some way to get Galina to the front, but there must have been fully two thousand people in the square, shoulder to shoulder with no gaps between them, and it was impossible. In the end she just lifted Galina onto her shoulders and got as close as she could.

A huge cheer went up before they had waited for much more than ten minutes. Even though Tanya was fairly tall she couldn't see much; there were too many taller people and hats between her and the theatre to do so. She thought she saw someone wave, but it might have just been one of the policemen controlling the crowd, signalling for them to keep back, and after only a few minutes the crowd began to disperse, the pilots apparently inside the building.

Tanya let Galina down and rolled her aching shoulders as she smiled wryly at her sister. 'Did you see anything?'

'Yes!' Galina nodded, but then she frowned and shrugged. 'Actually, I don't know. I think it was them, but they had big black coats on and those silly high hats. It could have been anyone.' For a long moment she looked down at the picture book she'd been clutching in her hands since they'd left home, but then she put it in her bag and hefted it onto her shoulder. She smiled up at Tanya. 'It doesn't matter, because my big sister is going to get me the autographs of all of the Wolfpack instead.'

'I'll see what I can do.' Tanya laughed and held out her hand. 'Come on, let's go.'

The girl took her hand and together they started back towards their grandfather's flat.

Tanya came to a halt after only a few paces, though, and sighed. Galina had tried to make it look like she was alright, but she obviously wasn't; her disappointment was evident in every heavy step she took away from the theatre.

Galina looked up at her in puzzlement. 'What are we doing, Tanyusha? Why have we stopped?'

Tanya didn't answer, but just gazed around the square, then at the theatre. She squatted down in front of the girl and looked her in the eyes. 'Do you remember what babushka taught you last summer in Novosibirsk?'

The family had been spending their summers in Siberia since before anybody could remember. The wooden lodge in the forest was where the older generation of her mother's family had always retired and it was where their maternal grandmother now lived. Traditionally, the older members of the family would take the younger ones out into the forest for "hunting" trips and hand them down the lessons which had been handed down to them over countless generations, not just on survival in the wilds, but of life. Tanya had been going out on the month-long trips with her grandmother and, when he was still alive, her grandfather, since she'd been Galina's age, and Galina had joined them for the first time that last summer.

That training had already proven invaluable to Tanya in her military career and it would serve them well now.

Galina's forehead creased slightly as she thought back and eventually nodded. 'I think so.' She wrapped her hands around her own neck and crossed her eyes as she made a choking sound.

Tanya laughed. 'Not that bit, silly!' she slapped her younger sister on the arm, 'the bit about sneaking around, especially in places you shouldn't be.'

The girl shook her head and tried to look innocent, like she didn't know what Tanya was talking about, but she knew she did; Tanya had caught her sneaking around the local *banya* in Moscow too many times, trying to snaffle snacks before their mother told her she could have them.

Galina giggled at Tanya's knowing look, then recited one of the most important lessons their grandmother had imparted to them. 'Look like you belong and people will assume you do.'

Tanya nodded. 'That's right - whenever you are hunting, whether it is for animals, food, people, or whatever, and whether you're in the forest or the city, success depends on fitting in with your surroundings.' She pointed at the theatre. 'Let's go and see how well you can hunt autographs in there, shall we?'

Galina looked at her, then glanced over her shoulder at the theatre, then turned back again. 'You mean...?'

Tanya nodded. 'Yes. We're going to crash a ballet.'

The sisters walked through the main doors of the theatre. Just inside were a couple of men in black suits, waiters, holding trays with drinks.

The men eyed them sceptically, but before they could say anything, Tanya grabbed a glass of wine for herself and a juice for Galina.

'Thank you.' She gave the man a brief smile, then walked away into the crowd of people in the lobby area, not giving him a chance to question her.

She led Galina to the side of the room, away from the doors, where there was a long table set with food. There was a little bit of space around it and Tanya was able to survey the crowd discreetly while she put some of the tiny pieces of tarts and other unidentifiable delicacies on a plate for Galina, who began devouring them hungrily. The Misfit pilots were easy enough to pick out of the crowd, not so much by the way they were dressed in black fur coats, but because they just looked so *uncomfortable* and out of place. One, who was probably the leader, was in the middle of the room speaking to a few officious-looking men, but the rest were standing in a group at the back of the room, near the stairs which led to the auditorium, conversing among themselves. They were surrounded by the ballet audience, who seemed to be treating them more as part of the show than as guests, talking about them, rather than to them.

'How are we going to get my autographs, Tanyusha?'

'I don't know, yet, Galichka.'

Tanya looked at the pilots again, wondering if any of them would be approachable - she had some English she could use for basic conversation, but she couldn't just push her way through the crowd and walk up to them without an excuse; if she were rejected, or even looked at funny, the security guards surrounding them would pounce on her and Galina wouldn't get her signatures.

Despite the confidence she was projecting and Galina's best efforts to look like the child of aristocracy, her junior officer's uniform and her sister's threadbare hand-me-down clothes stood out from the finery around them and out of the corner of her eyes she saw one of the waiters from the door stalking towards them with a security guard in tow. There was nothing else to do, she was going to have to take the risk of approaching the Misfits in the open without any cover. She took a deep breath and mentally prepared herself, but, before she could move, one of the male pilots glanced in her direction.

Their eyes met and he smiled at her.

That was all she needed. She downed the rest of her drink, took Galina's plate from her and chucked it onto the buffet table, then grabbed her hand.

'Stay close.'

She dived into the crowd and began weaving her way through them, dragging Galina behind her. She kept her eyes focussed firmly on her prey, though, assessing him as she went, trying to get some clue as to how to handle him best. The British pilot was watching her approach and his cheeky, confident smile spoke volumes to her. It seemed that he was the kind of man who was used to the attention of women and sought it out whenever he could. Rather than put her off, though, she smiled inwardly; that was precisely the kind of man she needed at that moment and, as she broke through the circle of people surrounding the pilots and closed the last couple of steps to him, she gave him her most seductive smile in return, the one her grandmother had made her practice.

'Hello.'

'Hello.' He was an inch or so shorter than her, with dark blonde hair and a deep tan, and there was an accent to his English that she wasn't expert enough to place.

'My name is Tatiana. How do you do?'

The man laughed at her formality, but not unkindly. 'I'm Bruce. Pleased to meet you.' His eyes flicked to her uniform briefly and she saw him take in the wings on her chest, a chest which she wished was just a little bit more prominent right then, so that she could better guarantee his continued interest in her for Galina's sake. 'You're a pilot?'

She nodded. 'I am.'

'What a coincidence - so am I!' He laughed again.

'Really?' She fluttered her eyelashes at him, continuing to show interest in him, despite the fact that she really wasn't.

Galina snorted in derision at the display - she was still too young to have received those lessons from grandmother - and she had to restrain herself from slapping her on the shoulder to stop her from spoiling things. As it was, the noise caught the pilot's attention and he smiled down at the young girl.

'Is this your daughter?'

'Oh, no! Silly!' Tanya laughed delicately and slapped Bruce on the arm gently, earning herself an amused look from Galina. 'She's my younger, very annoying, sister, Galina.'

'Ah! Hello, Galina.' The pilot beamed, very obviously glad, and greeted the girl, before turning back to Tanya. He saw the empty glass in her hand. 'Here, let me get you another.'

The waiter from before had followed her and had been slowly approaching, waiting for an opportunity to jump in and ask her to leave, but he was taken by surprise when the pilot grabbed two vodkas and a juice from his tray and then turned his back on him, blocking him out.

Bruce gallantly handed the juice to Galina, then one of the vodkas to her.

'Thank you.' She held out the glass for him to chink his own against and he obliged with another laugh.

'Cheers!'

'Cheers!' She took a deep gulp and smacked her lips before smiling at him. 'Bruce. Can I ask you a favour, please?'

The pilot beamed. 'Of course, Tatiana. Anything.'

'My sister is a bit of a fan of the Misfits. Do you think she could have your autograph?'

The man looked surprised and slightly disappointed by the mundane request, but he quickly hid it. 'Of course!' He winked. 'Would you like one too?'

'Yes please!' She bat her eyelashes again and ignored Galina's scornful reaction.

She took Galina's picture book and a pen from her and handed them across.

As he flicked through the book he chuckled again and she found that she was warming to him, despite herself. His laughter was an extremely pleasant sound and the way his mouth widened when he did so creased the corners of his eyes and turned his already handsome face into an extremely attractive one. She felt her heart quicken against her will and had to force herself to concentrate on what she was doing; they had almost achieved their objective and it would ruin everything if she got distracted now.

The man eventually found what he was looking for - the page with what must have been his aircraft - and he signed it with a flourish, before turning to the man next to him and tapping him on the shoulder, interrupting his conversation. 'Here, Monty, sign this would you and pass it around?'

The other pilot, an older man with a bald head, took the book and frowned at it, puzzled, but then saw Galina watching him hopefully and smiled. 'Righty ho!' He turned the pages until he found his aircraft, then signed it and gave it to the next pilot.

Tanya watched Galina for a moment, as she followed her book around the Misfits, not letting it out of her sight for an instant, before turning back to Bruce.

'Thank you for that. You've made her very happy.'

'It was my pleasure. So...'

A bell rang, announcing that it was only a few minutes to the commencement of the ballet, cutting him off before he could say anything else and the men and women around them started drifting away towards the auditorium.

'Ladies and Gentlemen, if you would follow me, please?' A young Palace Guard officer appeared and called out to the Misfits, waving at them for them to go with him.

Bruce smiled. 'Looks like we have to go.'

'Me too.' Tanya looked around nervously. The crowd was thinning out considerably and there suddenly seemed to be a lot more waiters and security men and nowhere to hide from them. It was time to find a side door and leave.

'I know!' Bruce exclaimed. 'Why don't you sit with us? You're missing Abby's signature anyway, so you'll have to come with us to get it and I still haven't given you my autograph.'

'Really?' Tanya glanced at Galina. She had returned and was listening to them, clutching her book to herself and grinning widely. She didn't understand English, but Bruce's gestures had been quite clear and she understandably looked excited at the prospect of watching the ballet with the pilots. It would be a huge risk for Tanya, though; if she were caught she could very easily be grounded before she'd even had her first combat flight.

In the end, Tanya decided that she didn't care about the extra risk; Galina was looking so happy and it would be something she would remember it for the rest of her life.

'That would be lovely, thank you, Bruce.'

A few minutes later, the sisters were sitting in the Tsar's box with the Misfits and a few high ranking Muscovite dignitaries. They had gotten a few strange looks when they had entered, but Bruce had pulled Tanya in close and Galina had wormed her way between a couple of the female pilots and nothing had been said. The young girl was even now sitting in the front row of the box between the two pilots - a diminutive redhead and a tall blonde - a look of sublime happiness on her face. Tanya, in the meantime, was sitting with Bruce in the back row. He had slipped his hand into hers with a familiarity she wasn't quite comfortable with, but she let him get away with it; it was harmless and besides, it was a small price to pay for Galina.

The ballet was good, excellent in fact, but Tanya found that she couldn't quite relax enough to enjoy it properly. Galina had the time of her life, though, dividing her attention almost equally between the dancers on the stage and the men and women around her. It was over too soon, though, Coppélia being far shorter than something like Swan

Lake, for example, and the guard officer returned to take the pilots backstage.

Before he could stand up, Tanya gently put her hand on Bruce's arm to hold him in place, then leaned over and kissed him. 'Thank you. That was wonderful.'

'You're welcome.' The pilot gave her a seductive smile which looked just as practised as her own. 'Would you like to have a drink, later?'

She nodded with a smile. 'I would love to.' She squeezed his hand, feeling distinctly sorry for lying to him, then stood up and joined the queue to leave the box.

The sisters accompanied the pilots down the staircase that led directly to the stage, but Tanya drifted away from Bruce as soon as she could and got hold of Galina. She knew there was an exit for the artists, the stage door, and, while the dancers were being introduced and everybody's attention was on the Misfits, they slipped out into the street. They went and sat in a cafe across the square at a table in the window, through which they could see the theatre and the big black autocars, waiting to take the Misfits away.

Tanya ordered tea and a few cakes, using the last of her pay to treat Galina, who, once again, stuffed the food into her mouth as if there were no tomorrow.

'Did you get everybody's autograph?'

Galina nodded enthusiastically. 'Everybody's! Including the leader, Abigail Lennox. And Scarlet gave me this as well.'

Galina took her picture book out of her bag, handling it now as if it were a religious relic, and opened it to reveal a set of RAC pilot's wings. They were the wings that the British wore on their dress uniforms, not their flightsuits or normal uniforms, and instead of being just cotton thread, the wings themselves were picked out in brass, while the crown and laurel wreath were real gold wire.

'Oh, wow.' Tanya leaned across the table to get a closer look at them. 'Which one was Scarlet? The blonde or the redhead?'

'The redhead.' Galina smiled. 'She was funny. I couldn't understand a word of what she was saying, but she made me laugh anyway by the way she spoke.'

Tanya laughed, but then looked up as movement caught her eye.

'There they are!' Despite having spent the last couple of hours with them, Galina was as excited to see the Misfits as she had been before and she pressed her face to the window to see better, misting it up with her breath.

Tanya didn't show it, but she searched the faces of the people coming out of the stage door just as enthusiastically, looking for Bruce, hoping that he wouldn't be too disappointed that she had disappeared.

She needn't have worried; he had a broad smile on his face when he came out and was laughing and joking with the bald pilot. She was quite pleased to see that he did, however, glance up and down the street, as if searching for something, and she was quite tempted to go to the cafe door and wave to him, but she resisted the temptation and instead just leaned back in her chair.

'Thank you, Bruce,' she murmured, smiling at the thought of the kiss she'd given him.

'What was that, Tanyusha?'

'Oh, nothing.' Tanya pushed her plate of cakes towards the girl. 'Come on, sit back down, there's more cake.'

Galina squealed in delight, flopped into her seat and took a huge bite, the Misfits forgotten. 'Thank you!'

Tanya laughed as crumbs sprayed everywhere and she made a show of wiping her face with her napkin.

Behind the girl, unseen by her, the pilots piled into the autocars and then drove off, leaving the square around the theatre empty, apart from the usual foot traffic, most, if not all of whom were oblivious to the warrior heroes who had just been driven past them.

'So,' said Galina around another mouthful. 'How are you going to get me those Wolfpack and Black Bear autographs?'

THE SILENT MAN

THE SILENT MAN

Sicily, 1st January 1941

I feel the eyes of the pilots, the latest batch of "Crimson Barons" (I forget if they're the third or fourth lot) on me as I walk across the mess with a tray of drinks from the bar. They see only a servant, one who caters to Hans Gruber's every whim, no matter how ridiculous. They see a toady, a sycophant, someone to be ignored at best and despised at worst. They think that I will report any indiscretion or insubordination of theirs that I witness back to my "master".

They couldn't be more wrong. About everything.

They are so proud to be part of this squadron, to wear that red lanyard over their shoulder. They think they have been lifted above the common Fliegertruppe pilots. They think they were chosen because they were the best available.

I know differently.

And I also know for certain, better than anyone, that the great Baron von Richthofen would barrel roll in his grave if he knew how his legend and his image had been appropriated by this clown and the inferior pilots he likes to surround himself with.

I was close with my cousin. More or less of an age, we learnt to fly together. However, while I was a good pilot, excellent even, I was overshadowed by him. Everyone was.

When the war broke out we naturally both became pilots.

His story is well known, mine isn't, and that anonymity, combined with my knowledge of warfare in the skies, meant that I was the ideal choice for the Kaiser when he needed someone to keep an eye on Gruber's activities.

The Kaiser has loved all things to do with flying since he was a boy and I was introduced to him at the Berlin Flying Club as the only surviving male relative of the legend that had been Manfred von Richthofen. I told him tales of Manny, of what kind of man he was and how he had flown, of how he had been a true knight of the sky. Eventually he and I became friends of sorts and after he ascended the throne he conferred on me the title of *Freiherr* which my cousin had had. Then, when the Bertha Berg was launched I agreed to become his spy and enter into Gruber's service, taking the name "Friedrich Lang" to further keep my identity a secret.

If only I'd known just how odious the task would be.

The deck I'm walking across is tilted, just another symptom of how all is not as it should be aboard the Bertha Berg. As is the view through the floor to ceiling windows of the Barons' mess.

Since the day the grand airship had been launched, the only view through the windows had been the endless sky, but now there are trees, fields, and even the low mountains of the Hyblaean range outside.

The airship has been brought low by Gruber and his insistence on having pilots as slaves to wind the springs. If he'd just had army grunts do it, like he'd been instructed, it would have been fine, but pilots were among the most intelligent men and women the enemy had to offer, so of course they would find a way to escape, and his shameful taunting of a gallant enemy, Lord Drake, had given them the opportunity.

That was something Manny would never have done. Those enemy pilots who survived him shooting them down were brought to his mess and treated as men, as warriors, as honoured guests. He had no need to *force* them to acknowledge his superiority because everyone already *knew* he was the best in the air.

It had only been thanks to the heroism of the naval personnel on board that Bertha had survived at all. At the first sign of trouble, Gruber had taken to the skies in his private aircraft and flown to a base in Sicily, leaving the naval crew to subdue the rebellious pilots and crash-land the stricken ship on the east coast of the island. He hadn't returned until the airship had been righted, propped up with a scaffold and declared safe.

My report on the events of Christmas Day is already winging its way to Berlin on one of the daily supply aircraft. We will have to see how the Kaiser reacts to this latest debacle, but I don't think it will prompt him to act; the slavery of the prisoners of war in the bowels of the Bertha is not something that the public has been made aware of - they wouldn't exactly approve - so a revolt among them will have to be hushed up.

I snarl at the thought of Gruber going unpunished once more, losing my composure for a moment in an extremely rare slip and earning a startled look from one of the overly made up women who have swarmed on board for the evening. I control myself immediately, though, and resume my impassive walk towards the group of people at the far end of the enormous room.

It is New Year's Day and the mess is bedecked for a celebration that the people who work on Bertha do not particularly feel like having. Gruber has never cared about them, though, and has brought in Italians for the occasion. *They* care nothing about the circumstances that put Bertha on the ground, have absolutely no qualms about drinking his wine and eating his food, and for once he actually has a truly appreciative audience, not just one who listens to him because they have to and pretends to agree with him.

Perhaps that will encourage him to open up and say something that he shouldn't, something that will push the Kaiser just a little too far, or that can be used against him at a later date if need be.

Kaiser Wilhelm is only too aware that Gruber will lose his value as a figurehead if he is defeated too many times and he has promised me the leadership of the Crimson Barons when the time comes to replace him. It is true that I'm far older than most pilots, but I have more skill than all these upstarts put together and my von Richthofen name will make me a more than acceptable replacement in the eyes of the public, especially when Gruber's American leanings and unhealthy obsession with an enemy pilot are revealed.

Finally someone who actually deserves the attention and acclaim of the people will receive it.

I hope that Misfit Squadron come to Malta soon. You'd think that all I've witnessed would be enough to have Gruber at least stripped of his command, if not his rank, but apparently, while he is still the darling of the people, he has to be kept in place and given every resource available, so that he cannot complain that the Kaiser is not supporting him. However, yet another humiliation at the hands of the British squadron should give the Kaiser exactly the excuse he needs to have him removed.

Until then, though, I am stuck kowtowing to this megalomaniacal imbecile.

I give him his drink without a word, keeping my face impassive so as not to show my contempt of him, then step back to watch and listen.

RELENTLESS

RELENTLESS

London, January 21st 1941

King George VI and his Queen Consort, Elizabeth, had been enjoying a rare quiet evening, without any air-raid warnings, with their daughters, Margaret and Elizabeth, in their private sitting room in Buckingham Palace, when the window shattered and two black bat-like creatures burst through the red velvet curtains to land in a shower of glass.

There was a scream from Margaret as her father snatched her from the floor at his feet, where she'd been playing with her toy horse, but the sound was instantly drowned out by the deafening blare of the machine guns of the Royal Guards, standing unobtrusively in the corners of the room. The shots had no apparent effect, though, and the black creatures didn't even flinch the impacts, they just slowly straightened from their crouches, folding their wings as they lifted their own weapons. One swivelled to track the King and Queen, but the other turned towards their eldest child, Elizabeth, sitting behind her school desk on the other side of the room.

Liz had been sketching Gwen Stone's new aircraft, Excalibur, which she'd seen take her maiden flight the week before, in an effort to understand how it was so good. Even though she'd constructed a couple of aircraft herself, she just couldn't get the feel of them, something which seemed to just come naturally to Gwen and so many other designers. She would dearly have loved to have spent more time with her, picking her brain and trying to find out how she did it, but she was gone; the Misfits had just been sent out on another perilous mission, this time to Malta. They always seemed to get the short end of the stick, but, of any of father's pet projects, they were the best positioned and capable of dealing with the danger and coming back alive.

It was an extremely pleasant and exceedingly interesting way to spend a quiet evening with her family, but all thoughts of flight had flown in the face of this new situation.

Her analytical mind worked overtime as she watched the violence taking place around her, taking note of various things, such as that the projectiles from the guards' weapons had seemed to be absorbed rather than deflected by the black armour the attackers were wearing, meaning it wasn't conventional, and that the eyes in their featureless masks were softly glowing red, which was possibly a sign that they were mechanicals, or perhaps some kind of vision enhancement. The armour and masks also effectively concealed the identity of the creatures. They were bipedal and the size of large men, but whether they were actually human, automatons, or something else - there had been talk of supernatural experiments being carried out by unsavoury men at the behest of Kaiser Wilhelm III - there was no way to tell.

Those observations were only her initial ones, made in the couple of seconds after the chaos began, but it didn't look like she was going to be afforded the time to make any more.

She watched as the barrel of the rifle swung towards her, foreshortening until it disappeared entirely and the only thing left was a black hole.

Something swept in front of her, blocking her vision of the weapon, just as the room filled with a chattering clash, which seemed even louder than the previous gunfire and she flinched back, almost overbalancing in her seat. It was a man - the guard who had been standing over her shoulder had leapt forward to cover her with his body. He was wearing armour, but it was ceremonial and it wasn't nearly enough to save his life. It did prevent the bullets from passing directly through his body and hitting her, though.

Blood splattered her desk, covering the paper in front of her, and struck her full in the face and upper body, but even then she didn't scream - afterwards she was very proud of that fact, that even when experiencing her first taste of death and danger she didn't cry out. The warm liquid and the coppery taste in her mouth did however spur her into action like the threat to her life hadn't.

As the guard groaned and began to collapse backwards onto her desk, Liz slipped sideways out of her seat to the floor and crawled behind an armchair. She was fully aware that it wouldn't provide any protection from the bullets, but it would serve to hide her from the attacker's sight for a few seconds while she decided what to do.

There was another scream, this time a woman's not a child's, and she couldn't help but peer around the chair to see what was happening.

Her parents and Margaret were cowering across the room behind a shield of three guards. The two men and one woman were firing at the attacker, holding it back momentarily, but they were cornered and their weapons were still proving ineffective. It was only a matter of time before first they, then the Royal Family were gunned down. Even as she watched, the creature opened fire and the first of the brave men was thrown backwards, his golden breastplate rent and red liquid spraying an absurd distance to splatter walls, ceiling and furniture alike.

Her father looked up in that moment and his gaze found hers. She saw despair in his eyes, and it shook her to the core, but it was instantly replaced by the toughness that she was more accustomed to and, beyond all her expectations, he smiled.

GO!

The mouthed word sent her spinning away and she scrambled for the concealed door in the wall behind her.

Bullets struck above her head, showering her with pieces of wallpaper-covered plaster, but then she was through. The door swung shut behind her as she stumbled and fell sprawling in the antechamber beyond, skinning her knees painfully under her woollen skirt.

'Elizabeth?'

Liz groaned and looked up to find the nanny, Beatrice, gazing at her in puzzlement from the armchair by the fire where she was accustomed to snoozing while her charges were with their parents, having "quality time" as she put it. She was almost completely deaf and mustn't have heard the uproar from beyond the thick door.

'What's happ…? My, God! Are you hurt?'

The old woman's eyes widened in shock and Liz realised that she must look quite awful, lying on the floor, covered in the guard's blood.

Beatrice struggled to get out of her chair with the undoubted intention of moving to help her, but Liz was quicker. She scrambled up and closed the distance to the old woman at a run and grabbed her hand.

'Nanny, come…'

Any argument she might have used to persuade the woman to flee with her on arthritic legs was cut off by a bang as the door slammed against the wall.

The old woman's eyes widened in alarm as she looked over Liz's shoulder.

Two bony, but surprisingly strong hands grabbed Liz painfully by the elbows and she found herself manoeuvred behind her venerable nanny. 'Run, darling girl.'

The whispered words were as good as a command and Liz found her legs obeying, taking her towards the doors on the other side of the room as fast as her stockinged feet could go.

Behind her, Beatrice's voice rang out, strong and clear as it hadn't been in years. 'You leave my Lilibet alone you big...!'

A loud report covered whatever name the usually reserved lady was going to call the creature and Liz heard a gasp. She cringed, expecting another gunshot to ring out at any moment, the gunshot that would hit her and take her life, but when it didn't come she looked over her shoulder.

Despite the huge red stain on the back of her grey dress, Nanny Beatrice was still on her feet. She had her hands wrapped around the creature's gun and, try as he might, he couldn't free it. The old woman's strength could only last so long, though, and eventually her legs gave out beneath her, but she still maintained her grip on the gun, dragging it downwards with her.

Red eyes lifted from the broken body on the floor as the gun finally came free, but she was across the room now and she burst through the gilt double doors and into one of the long connecting corridors.

Liz sprinted along the thick carpet, past the portraits on the walls, her eyes fixed on the door at the far end, but her mind on the Royal Guard barracks four rooms past them.

She was less than half-way to them when the doors behind her were kicked open with a crash.

She was never going to make it.

There was an opening to her left and she swerved into it as the first shot rang out. Something tugged at her sleeve and she cried out as she was pulled off balance and crashed into the wall, upsetting a side table and sending a vase, hopefully not too expensive, but probably horribly so, crashing to the floor. Somehow she kept her feet, though, spinning and stumbling in a way that probably would have given her dance teacher an apoplexy, and she surged forwards again towards the end of the, thankfully short, corridor.

She burst through the heavy wooden door at the end and found herself in a wide atrium.

Far too late she realised that the turning led to the Brunel Tower, which usually wouldn't have been a bad thing, except for the fact that all exits from it, apart from the one she'd come through, had been locked and barricaded for security purposes at the start of the war.

The tower was huge and afforded innumerable hiding places, but she was essentially trapped in it.

Ignoring the splendid view through the glass and iron latticework of the winter sunset over the snow-covered lawns of the palace garden, she ran to the thick column in the middle of the room and stabbed at the button which called the lifts - she could go to her personal laboratory on the tenth floor; there were plenty of places to hide there.

There was a whir of spinning wheels and cogs then the door on her left began to slide open, accompanied by the heavenly sound of a chord played by a church organ as the compressed air created by the lift's previous arrival was released through the pipes installed by Handel almost a century ago.

Liz leapt through the gap as soon as it was wide enough for her and pressed the button to take her to the tenth floor, then the one that closed the doors.

Far too slowly for her liking, the doors stopped opening, then reversed their course.

They ground to a halt after a couple of seconds, though, when the lights in the lift went out.

'No, no, no!'

She jabbed at the button to close the doors. Even though the lights in the atrium had also gone off and she knew that the electricity to the Tower must have been cut off, meaning that the lift couldn't possibly obey her command, she kept pushing it over and over.

After several long seconds she managed to stop herself and she rested her forehead against the cold copper doors, fighting to calm down.

'You're acting irrationally, Liz,' she told herself out loud, 'that's one of the first signs of panic - you've heard that often enough. Pull yourself together, you don't have time for this.'

She took a deep, calming breath, then forced herself into movement.

She pushed her way through the gap in the doors and went along the wall to a wooden door. It opened with a squeal of hinges which made her jump and she laughed nervously; nobody ever used the stairs and it probably hadn't been touched in months, if not years. She pushed the door closed behind her, wincing as it squealed again, seemingly far louder now that she was expecting it.

She'd thought the atrium had been dark, but it had been positively bright in comparison to the stairwell - even the emergency lights were dark - and she spent some of her valuable time fumbling around for a lock before realising that something that doubled as an escape route in case of fire wouldn't have one.

She swore under her breath, using one of the delightfully provincial phrases that she'd heard the irrepressible Scarlet Flynn using at the Midwinter celebration a few weeks before, then edged her way towards the stairs. Even with all her care she still managed to stub her toe on the unseen step and dropped to her bloody knees. The sudden pain spurred her like her fear hadn't and she groped at the wall, searching for a handrail. She found it and used it to pull herself to her feet, then began her climb.

She took it slowly at first, not wanting to waste time or energy by tripping or slipping on the carpet, but as she got a feel for the height of the steps she got into a rhythm and began moving quicker. She didn't move so quickly that she would have trouble making it to the tenth floor, though; she had no illusions about her fitness and knew she was already tired after a long day and the sprint through the palace.

When her father had allocated her a room in the tower for her experiments she had taken time to study the architectural plans, so she knew she needed to go up twenty-four flights of stairs to reach her laboratory - six flights to reach the first floor, because of the high-ceilinged atrium, then two flights for each subsequent floor. She had gone up eight flights, a third of the distance, when there was a squeal as the door below opened, then another as it closed again.

She stopped dead, not wanting to make any noise that would give herself away, then shuffled as quietly as she could to the safety railing on the inside of the spiralling staircase.

There wasn't much space between the column containing the lift and the stairs, perhaps two feet, but that was enough for her to be able to lean over and peer down.

For what seemed like several minutes - her father wouldn't let her wear her Frobisher chronograph around the palace so she had no idea exactly how long - there was just blackness, and the only sound was her own laboured breathing. She was beginning to think that the creature must have just looked into the stairwell and, seeing nothing, gone to search elsewhere. She was just about to turn away and continue her climb when her she thought she detected a change in the quality of the darkness. A faint lightening. A red glow.

She strained her ears trying to hear something, sure that, if it were the creature, then it was so large that its footfalls would be easily audible in the absolute silence, but there was nothing.

She was ready to dismiss the glow as just her eyes playing tricks on her, but then suddenly two bright points of red light appeared in the gap, only a few floors below her.

She gasped and staggered back, tripping as her foot missed the step. She desperately flung out an arm and twisted, grasping for the railing along the wall. She cried out when her shoulder wrenched painfully, but she managed to catch her fall before she tumbled downwards.

Cruel, malicious, definitely human laughter filled the stairwell, reverberating from the walls, surrounding her, but when it faded there was again silence.

Something broke in her then, snapping like a twig, and she lost her careful control as some primal instinct to flee awoke in her, overriding her intellect. She clambered to her feet and began running up the stairs, stumbling and scrabbling as she missed her footing every few steps.

The creature, the *man* was never going to give up. She couldn't escape it, it would find her, whatever she did. Her parents and sister were probably already dead and it wasn't going to stop until she was too.

She ran and ran, even as her lungs threatened to burst, even as her legs turned to jelly beneath her and she was spending more time on her hands and knees than she was on her feet.

Even in her panic, some part of her kept track of the number of turns she took and when she reached the tenth floor she staggered to the door and collapsed against it. She clawed for the handle, breaking at least a couple of her nails on the tiled wall and the door edge before she found it. Without looking back, she went through and stumbled down the short hallway, past the two storerooms, to the door to her private space.

She turned the handle and pushed against the door, slapping it when it didn't open, throwing her shoulder into it painfully. She began to cry in frustration and slapped it again, cursing it, before belatedly realising that she hadn't put her code into the keypad.

Her trembling fingers only just managed to press the correct numbers and she sobbed in relief as there was a solid *clunk* and the door swung open. She leapt through and grabbed the thick door, slamming it shut behind her, hearing the loud click as it locked again.

She was under no illusion that the door would hold the creature for very long, but it would give her precious moments to do...

What?

Why did I come here?

In the familiar surroundings, Liz's mind gradually became calmed and focussed, eventually taking on the state that it was accustomed to take when in this room.

Her eyes darted this way and that, moving from one of her dozens of experiments to another in the huge room, which took up almost the entire tenth floor, searching for inspiration. There was very little light coming through the windows now the sun had gone down completely and the workbenches around her were not much more than shadows, but she didn't need to see them to know exactly what was on them.

Her gaze briefly came to rest on the emergency glidewings hanging by the windows on the far side of the room. They were supposed to be for escape in the event of a fire, but she'd been toying with them as part of her investigation of flight and they were partially dismantled. She might be able to put them together in time to jump, though...

She immediately dismissed the idea; not only would the man find her before she could repair them, but he was wearing glidewings himself and would undoubtedly catch her.

She continued her scan of the room, but for the life of her, quite literally, she couldn't work out why her instincts had brought her to her laboratory instead of going up to the top of the tower where there were dozens of soldiers manning the anti-aircraft guns.

The crash of the stairwell door opening announced the arrival of the man on her floor.

She was out of time.

A fresh jolt of fear sent adrenaline surging through her, sharpening her mind further, and she began to look beyond the experiments themselves, beyond the unfinished gadgets, machines and weapons to the raw materials with which they were fabricated and even the room itself.

Another crash startled her out of her thought process almost immediately, though, and she looked towards the door, expecting to see it gaping open, but it had been one of the flimsy storeroom doors taking the brunt of the attacker's ire and she smiled; it was good to know that he wasn't omnipotent, that he wasn't tracking her - he had just known, somehow, that she would head for her laboratory.

You're too predictable, Your Highness.

As she scrambled around the room, grabbing a pair of protective gloves from the nearest table and slipping them on, she could almost hear the voice of her fencing instructor, Major Cockburn, chiding her for always behaving in a logical fashion. It served her admirably in most things, but it made her predictable when she was fighting, whether it were fisticuffs or fencing, and might well get her killed that evening. Still, if *anything* was going to get her out of the bother she was in, it was her logical...

Acid!

The idea sprang into her mind and she broke into a run just as another bang announced the man breaking down the door of the second storeroom. She had a supply of sulphuric acid in the chemical store at the side of the room for use in simple batteries and alchemical experiments, it would be easy enough to throw the glass bottle at the man and then...

Her hand was already on the cupboard door when she realised it wouldn't work, the man's body was completely covered with an armour of an unknown type - even if the acid ate through it, which wasn't guaranteed, he would have plenty of time to shoot her, then take it off before it ever got near his skin.

What else?

After seeing how ineffectual the weapons of the guards had been, projectile weapons were out, not that she had any anyway; her interests ran more to the mechanical and electrical, but...

The door to the laboratory was struck by a heavy object. And again after a few seconds. And again. Against all expectations it held and the pounding stopped after only a few more impacts - the man evidently realising that what he was doing wasn't working.

When she'd moved into the room, her father had told her that the walls and doors of all the work spaces in the tower had been constructed to be capable of withstanding a moderate explosion, that the windows were designed to provide a release for any blast and were made of a plastic polymer, rather than glass, so as not to spray razor-sharp shards over the surrounding area. At the time she'd half thought he was joking. She was extremely glad he hadn't been.

How long would the door withstand the battering, though? And was there *anything* she could prepare in the meantime which would stop the man when he got through? Because she had no illusions as to the fact that he *would* get in sooner or later.

She doubted it.

She closed her eyes and rested her forehead against the wall next to the chemical cupboard, feeling the cold, sharp edges of one of the electrical sockets, which were liberally scattered around the room, pressing into her skin. She took a deep breath then let it out as a sigh.

Part of her wanted to just curl up on the floor, close her eyes and wait for the end. She had done all she could and besides, she was just a fourteen-year-old and the man outside her door was a professional killer, probably one of the best the Prussians had, given the importance of the mission, so there would be no shame in giving up.

That was only a very small part of her, though. Her mind, her desire to one day be a Misfit, her will to live and above all her very *British* pigheadedness refused to let her.

She lifted her head from the cold metal and looked for the best place to hide. There were cupboards everywhere, under every desk, all of them large enough to hide her, and there were crawl spaces in a few of her machines she could, well, crawl into. That would only be prolonging the inevitable, though; he would find her eventually and she wasn't confident that help would arrive before he did.

No. Hiding would be as good as giving up. She needed to find something else to do.

But what? There isn't *anything!*

Her forehead was sore and she reached up to rub it, then stopped.

There *was* one thing she could do, but did she have enough time to set it up?

She glanced nervously at the door and, despite knowing that her plan was the best hope she had, she hesitated. Everything was still inexplicably quiet. She still had time to find a place to hide...

She forced the traitorous thought aside and began moving about the room, frantically connecting wires, throwing things on the floor, flicking switches.

A low humming began to fill the large space - her experiments and machines were all independently powered or connected to batteries that were kept fully charged by the wind turbines at the top of the tower, rather than the Tesla Generator in the palace basement, so that vital experiments wouldn't be ruined by any interruption in power.

A blast of gunfire accompanied by the thunder of impacts on wood sent Liz scrambling for shelter behind one of her solid wooden workbenches, but she immediately realised that, at least for the moment, the projectiles were being stopped by the door, so she steeled herself and went back to work.

The door was thick and reinforced with a metal plate, but it couldn't last long and all too soon splinters and almost spent bullets were flying across the room, shattering glassware and knocking over whatever they came across.

A beaker exploded next to Liz's head, showering her with fragments, and she screamed and ducked behind the nearest workbench, her hands over her head to protect herself.

For the first time in her life, she wished there was someone or something she could pray to; she only needed a little bit of good fortune, for the bullets careening around the room to not hit the wrong thing, or her, before she made the last couple of connections.

The irony of that didn't escape her.

The gunfire stopped abruptly, leaving her ears ringing, and she leapt up.

She made it only two steps before the door toppled, its hinges destroyed, and crashed onto the floor revealing two sinister red circles of light.

'Fun's over, girly.'

Liz dived into cover again, ignoring the fresh pain in her already punished knees and gave the last wire a twist, completing the circuit, then took a deep breath - it was time for the riskiest part of the plan.

She stood up.

The man immediately pointed his weapon at her, but she had been ready for it and ducked down again before he could open fire, going to all fours behind the bench. 'Wait! I give up! Just... before you kill me, please, tell me who sent you. Why are you here?'

Liz cringed, ashamed of how stupid she sounded; there was no doubt that the man was Prussian - if his actions weren't enough, his accent confirmed it - so he was here at the behest of the Kaiser or one of his minions, and as for his mission, well, that was equally obvious.

The man laughed. 'Ah! You British Royals! I don't know why the Kaiser wants all of you dead; you are all so inbred, so stupid!'

There was a clicking noise as the man walked into the room; while most of the palace, including the tower stairwell, was thickly carpeted, the floor in her laboratory was a hard resin that was resistant to damage, but which did nothing to muffle the sound of the man's boots.

'I have been sent by Kaiser Wilhelm to kill you, isn't it obvious?'

Of course it bloody is. 'I... I...' Liz stuttered, buying as much time as she could. 'But I'm just a child, I don't know anything about politics or the war. I don't know why you would want to kill me! Killing me won't change anything!'

The footsteps came closer.

'Ha ha! I have seen the newsreels of you and your father in parliament. I was in the audience when you made your speech at the opening of that ridiculous Misfit exhibition. You, like your father, mother and sister, are symbols for the people of this country. They are weak, and without you, they will lose hope, lose their will to fight, and we will take what is rightfully ours.'

A pair of shiny black boots rounded the corner of the bench and she looked up and met clear blue eyes. The man had pushed his mask back onto the top of his head, exposing a surprisingly young face that would have been handsome if it hadn't been twisted by a look of such intense hatred.

He smirked, looking down his sharp nose at her. 'But you know all that, of course. You were hoping to play me like the fool?'

She smiled. 'Actually, I have done. Sorry.'

That wasn't the reaction he'd expected or, as a bully, wanted, and he scowled and lifted the gun again, but then paused.

The humming of her machine had been steadily building, increasing in volume and pitch while they'd been talking and now it rose to a whistling shriek.

She had delayed just enough.

The man looked around nervously, taking in all the machines humming and whirring around the room. 'Vas ist das? What is that noise?'

Despite it being rather undignified, Liz had remained on all fours while she'd been speaking to the Prussian, but now she pushed herself up, raising her knees so that only her hands and feet, insulated in boots and gloves, were touching the huge sheet of copper she'd thrown on the floor behind the bench. The one which she had drawn the man towards and on which he was now standing.

'Oh, it's just a little something Kitty Wright and I have been working on. It's nothing to worry about. Not for me, anyway.'

The shriek, which sounded innocuous, like a kettle boiling, reached a painful volume, making Liz wince, but then it just cut off. It was replaced immediately, though, by a hideous gurgling noise and she squeezed her eyes shut, not wanting to see the results of her handiwork, as the current from her machine passed through the man's body, conducted so handily by the nails, or "blakeys", soldiers would insist on putting in their boots.

The noise stopped after a surprisingly short time and the Prussian fell to the floor, missing her by inches. She stood and moved to the machine, flicking switches to turn it off and send the remaining electrical power to ground, making sure that it was safe again.

She slowly became aware of a gentle sizzling noise coming from the floor behind her, accompanied by an all-too familiar smell and she glanced at the man, but instantly turned away again, her stomach turning.

No more bacon sandwiches, I swear! At least for a while.

Bodies were nothing new to her; she had accompanied her father on his visits to the bombed-out neighbourhoods of London, but the smell was, so she grabbed an insulating visor from a nearby bench and put it on before beginning to unfasten the man's glidewings.

Liz alighted in the quadrangle, in the middle of a group of red-clad Royal Guards, who just stared at her. She looked around incredulously, not quite believing that they were outside, standing around like lemons, instead of inside the palace, fighting to save her family.

'The King and Queen! An assassin! What are you all doing...?'

'Elizabeth!'

'Papa!' Liz spun towards the sound of the voice and staggered as the weight of the glidewings threatened to overbalance her. She almost stabbed a nearby soldier with one of the sharp tips before, cheeks burning, she thought to fold them in. She shrugged out of the straps, letting the pack fall to the ground, then ran to meet her father as he strode through the guards towards her.

She crashed into him, burying her head in his chest, breathing in the familiar scents of the wool of his suit and his cologne. His arms wrapped around her, pulling her to him, and the tension just flowed from her, along with whatever it had been that had kept her going. Her legs tried to collapse underneath her and tears began to come, but she summoned the last of her determination and put on a brave face, as she'd been taught all her life, then stepped back.

She straightened her clothing as best she could before looking up at him. 'Mother? And Margaret?'

He smiled and motioned towards the guard barracks that he'd appeared from. 'Inside, safe.'

'I thought you were all...' She swallowed, unable to finish.

'Many brave men and women died before the Prussian was stopped. Would you believe it took a tank in the end?' The King paused and glanced over the top of her head at the glidewings being collected by one of the soldiers. 'I take it the second assailant has been attended to?'

He turned a quizzical look on her and she gave him a half-smile and a shrug in return - all that she could really summon. 'I'm going to need some new equipment in my laboratory, I'm afraid I made a bit of a mess.'

The King laughed. 'I think the budget can stretch to that.'

'Thank you, father.' She nodded her gratitude, then shivered as a sudden breeze swept across the frozen courtyard.

The King saw and beckoned to one of the palace servants, waiting nearby with a blanket and steaming mug of tea. 'Come on, let's get you in front of a fire and you can tell us all about it.'

Liz allowed the servant to place the blanket around her shoulders, but refused the tea, preferring to clutch her father's arm with both hands instead as they walked towards the door of the barracks.

She yawned as exhaustion hit her like a steam wagon, but a sudden thought had her looking over her shoulder. 'Papa, may I keep the glidewings?'

REACHING
FOR THE SKIES

REACHING FOR THE SKIES

Transcript of the meeting between Commander of the Royal Aviator Corps Sir Douglas Beauregard Pewtall (DP) and Squadron Leader Lady Penelope Doris Bader Bagshot (PB), Whitehall, April 2nd 1941.

DP - Lady Penelope, do come in. You're looking well.

PB - Thank you, one does one's best to put on a brave face.

DP - Especially when one is so much in the public eye, as yourself.

PB - Precisely.

DP - Please, sit. Would you like tea?

PB - No thank you, Douglas, this isn't a social visit and I won't be taking up much of your time.

DP - Very well. To what do I owe the pleasure, then?

PB - I was wondering if you'd heard anything from Malta.

DP - Not since Basil asked me the same question - I assume he came at your instigation? When was that? The day before yesterday? You know we don't get regular reports from Malta and as I told him, we're not expecting anything back from Gibraltar for at least a week. Did you truly get all dressed up in your best uniform and come to London just for that?

PB - No, of course not.

DP - I didn't think so.

PB - Shall we get straight to it, then?

DP - By all means.

PB - I'd like to go back on active duty.

DP - Ha ha! Very funny! But you're a day late.

PB - I'm not joking.
DP - You're not?
PB - No.
DP - Really?
PB - Yes.
DP - But it's impossible!
PB - Why?
DP - What do you mean why?
PB - I mean - why?
DP - Well... Because you lost both your legs!
PB - Did you not see me walk in here?
DP - Yes, of course, but...
PB - But what, Douglas?
DP - Well, you know.
PB - No, I'm afraid I don't.
DP - Are you really going to make me spell it out for you, Penny?
PB - I think you ought to, yes.
DP - Well, it's just that... You're... You've...
PB - Yes?
DP - You're not fit!
PB - I could do some jumping jacks right here, or run up and down the corridor if you'd like.
DP - No that won't be....
PB - Or I could kick your arse.
DP - ...necessary. I'm sorry, what was that?
PB - I said, "I have a kick like a horse". Thanks to my new legs, that is.
DP - Oh... Right... I... No. There's no need for demonstrations. I actually meant not fit to fly. It's been, what? Six months since the, uh, accident?
PB - Six and a half.
DP - If I put you in an aircraft and you can't handle it...
PB - I've been flying for more than four months now.
DP - You've been...
PB - Close your mouth, Douglas, I'm not your dentist.
DP - Sorry. Um.
PB - Um?
DP - Well, I... There's a big difference between just flying and flying in combat. Six months isn't enough time...
PB - Six and a half.

DP - It's not enough time for you to have recovered mentally. When you face the enemy for the first time the shock might cause you to freeze up. You'd be killed.

PB - Do you question every new pilot in this way? Do you know how many of them die the first time you send them up? Either by "freezing" as you put it, or simply not being prepared.

DP - I do.

PB - Yet you still send them up.

DP - I have to.

PB - Then why treat me any differently?

DP - Because... Because you're... You're not just... Oh, for Victoria's sake, Penny, why can't you just take a posting on the ground? You've done your bit, more than most, why not leave it at that?

PB - Rest on my laurels, you mean?

DP - Exactly!

PB - You are British, aren't you Douglas? Because sometimes you don't sound it.

DP - That was uncalled for, Penelope.

PB - I know, I'm sorry, but I feel extremely strongly about this.

DP - I can see that, but it's just not going to happen, sorry. My conscience just won't allow me to put you back in a combat aircraft. Perhaps when we push back the Prussians we can find you a transport to fly...

PB - XXXXXXXXXXXXXXXXXX. *redacted for decency*

DP - Please don't be like that, I'm only doing this...

HRH - What oh!

DP - Your Majesty! What...

HRH - Please, don't bother getting up, Dougie, this isn't a formal visit. I just popped by the office to do some paperwork and someone told me Penny was here. I didn't believe it so I had to come and see for myself. My dear! How are you?

PB - Very well, thank you, George, darling.

HRH - Good, good! You are looking wonderful, I must say! And I suppose you're ready to get back on active duty?

PB - Oh, yes. That's why I'm here in fact. Douglas and I were just debating where my talents would be best put to use.

HRH - Splendid! That's the ticket! But do come and have tea before you get sent off to some faraway place, would you? It's been too long since you were at the palace and I know Elizabeth would dearly love to see you and pick your brains again. If you don't mind, of course.

Perhaps tomorrow? Bring Biffy and we'll make an occasion of it! And Dougie, make sure you give her a decent posting, would you? She deserves it!

DP - Er, yes, sir. Of course, sir.

HRH - There's a good chap. Well, I'll be off, then. Dougie. See you tomorrow, Penny!

PB - Looking forward to is, Georgy!

HRH - Toodle pip!

DP - Ahem, well... Let me see... I have a squadron who are just finishing their training and are due to go up to Scotland next week to get some time on Spits. You can take them and knock them into shape before they go on active duty on the south coast. How is that?

PB - That sounds just the ticket. Thank you, Douglas. Now, that wasn't so hard, was it?

Royal historian's note.

With the intervention of His Royal Highness King George VI, what had begun as just an informal conversation took on far greater meaning and several events of great significance in the Second Great War can be directly traced back to this single meeting. Some historians have even theorised that without the King's intervention that day the war may have been lost, or at least prolonged immeasurably, at great cost to the world as a whole.

MONTY

MONTY

It is with the deepest regret that The Times has to report that a second Misfit Squadron pilot has fallen in the course of duty while posted to Malta.

Aviator Lieutenant Montgomery Graham Fletcher, DAC, DAM was killed on this last 8th May while taking part in an assault on a classified Prussian objective and as such the precise details of his death have not been released.

F. Featherstonehaugh, 14th May 1941

OBITUARY

Aviator Lieutcnant Montgomcry Graham Fletcher, DAC*, DAM. 1908 - 1941

Montgomery Fletcher, "Monty" to all who knew him, was born to Walter Fletcher and Edith Towers on January 8th, 1908 in a circus caravan in a field near Lincoln. His mother, the daughter of the founders and owners of the *Towers's Flying Circus*, died in childbirth, and he was raised by his father.

Walter Fletcher had been an RAC pilot in The Great War and, like so many returning servicemen, had been unable to find work when the war ended. He answered an advertisement in a newspaper and joined the circus as a mechanic, but quickly earned a place for himself among the men and women who displayed their skills in the sky.

Monty joined his father in the air before he could walk, but it wasn't until he was four that he officially became part of the act, performing as a wing walker or serving as a rear-gunner during mock dogfights. However, by the time he was six, he was a more than capable pilot in his own right, which enabled them to expand their act considerably. The pair received excellent reviews and fast became audience favourites, prompting the circus to begin billing them as "The Flying Fletchers" and making them one of the star attractions.

The opening skit to their act was their most well-known. In it, Monty would pretend to have difficulty climbing up onto the wing in order to perform his wing walking duties. Walter would go up and lean down to offer his hand, but in the meantime the boy had clambered into the cockpit. Monty would then take off and fly the aircraft, performing acrobatics while his father comically held on as best as he could - although in reality he had used the distraction provided by Monty to attach himself to a safety wire, which was invisible to the spectators.

The skit was immortalised in the 1921 Charles Chaplin flyvie *The Scamp*, which won several IMP (*Imperial Motion Picture Academy*) awards, including "Best Aerial Stunt", with Monty acting as the stunt double of the titular character.

The Flying Fletchers were the most successful act the Towers's circus ever had, but after only three years, when Monty was nine, his father died, leaving him orphaned and he was taken into the care of his maternal grandparents, who had retired from taking an active part in running the circus, but still travelled with them.

Monty continued to work, only now as part of the main show, rather than one of the star attractions. He became one of the dogfighting pilots, taking on the personality of a diminutive, but brave, RAC officer with a comically large moustache, who stood up to the much larger enemies who sought to bully him. His father's aircraft became his and was repainted accordingly from its bright red colouring to brown and green RAC camouflage.

Monty's character struck a chord with British audiences, who not only loved to cheer for the underdog, but also saw him as representing Britain herself, with her eternal and often solitary struggle against forces which sought to limit freedom.

At fourteen, Monty became too tall to carry on the character, but by that time he'd had his success with *The Scamp* and was able to leave the circus and go to work as a full time stunt pilot for the studio. He was never completely content with the job, though, and when, in 1927, at the age of nineteen, he was involved in an accident that burned his scalp so that his hair only grew in patches, he returned to the circus as an adult performer.

While growing up, he'd spent as much or more time with the circus mechanics as he had in the air, learning about the maintenance and construction of the aircraft. He now put that knowledge, and the money he'd earned in the flyvies to good use, designing and constructing his own aircraft using the new spring technology.

Over the course of the next twelve years he divided his time between performing in the shows and studying aircraft design, refining his work until it culminated in Ballerina, the aircraft that caught Abigail Lennox's attention and which he brought with him when he joined the Royal Aviator Corps and Misfit Squadron.

Aviator Lieutenant Fletcher's time as a Misfit has been well-documented. While not one of the most well-known Misfit pilots, Monty was instrumental in their successes over France, Britain and Muscovy in first Ballerina, then Raptor, then finally Ghoul - the machine which he helped design and in which he died. He made thirty-two kills and won both the Distinguished Aviation Cross and the Distinguished Aviation medal.

He never married and is survived only by his maternal grandmother.

Note: As reported previously, the other fallen Misfit pilot, William MacShane, was posthumously awarded the Victoria Medal. There is no word as yet whether the same will be done for Aviator Lieutenant Fletcher.

MISSING,
PRESUMED DEAD

MISSING, PRESUMED DEAD

The Mediterranean Sea, somewhere between Sicily and Malta, 9th May 1941

Well, Chas, you were stupid and now you're dead.
'Yes, thank you, Berty, that's very helpful.'
I'm just saying.
Chastity banished the voice of her dead friend from her head and took stock of her surroundings for the umpteenth time in the last hour or so.

Unsurprisingly, nothing had changed. There was still only water in every direction as far as she could see, which wasn't exactly very far, with her head only six inches or so above the sea, bobbing up and down and shivering as the cold seeped into her.

She sighed and tilted her head back to stare up at the sky, but there was nothing to see there, either. The last of the aircraft had gone, the enemy raid having passed over a while ago, heading back to their bases in Sicily, and the trails of smoke and condensation they had left behind were already being shredded, blown to smithereens by the winds.

She sighed again.

Berty was right, even though she was just a voice in her head. She was, indeed, dead. Or at least *going* to die before too long.

And she had been stupid. Idiotic, actually. She had allowed herself to be shot down by Hans Gruber, served herself up on a platter in fact.

While the rest of the Misfits had been kept occupied by the other Barons, Gruber and three of his henchmen had swooped on Wright, Guseva, Farrier, and herself in their Spitsteams and she had tried to be clever. She knew they would expect her to break; it was the standard response to the situation, but instead she had just kept going straight and opened fire. It had worked, after a fashion, and she had shot down one of the Blutsaugers, but, unfortunately, in return she had found herself in what amounted to a ballistic projectile after her wings had been clipped off by cannon rounds from Gruber and one of his allies.

Under normal circumstances she would have been able to take to her glidewings and, if not make it back to dry land, at least get near to a boat which could pick her up - it was what she and many other British pilots had done before.

However, five things had conspired against her to make that impossible.

1) Her canopy had been damaged and she had to fight for quite a long time to get it open, so she was too low when she jumped to get anywhere with her glidewings.

2) The trajectory of her Spitsteam had taken her too far from Malta for the spotters on the coast to have seen her go down.

3) It had been too soon after the fight began for the naval launches to get to her.

4) No fishing boats had been within range to see her or pick her up.

5) Her radio had been destroyed, so there had been no chance to send a signal reporting her position.

All of which combined meant that she was stuck some twenty miles or so from Malta, probably not very near shipping lanes or fishing grounds, and with nothing she could do to change her circumstances except expire before slowly sinking into the sea.

Although, she might be particularly unlucky and a shark might wander by and finish things a bit quicker.

'*Are* there sharks in the Mediterranean, Berty?'

There was no answer from her friend, but the sea seemed to provide one, as the water boiled and churned about twenty yards to her left. It seemed like a bit too much of a disturbance to be a shark and there was no fin in evidence, but she didn't know much about sharks so it could still have been one. She actually quite hoped it would be a kraken; that would make her final moments a hell of a lot more interesting than just a big grey fish with sharp teeth and would be a much more worthy end for one of the bloody Misfits... even if there was nobody around to see it.

It wasn't a shark coming for her, or a kraken, or any of the other numerous guises the Dark Scythesman could take, according to the poem, but rather a very man-made metal monster.

An undersea boat. Thankfully, a British one.

A round hatch on the deck clanged open and a few sailors clambered out. One of them, an officer, lifted a speaking trumpet and shouted at her. 'Oi! You there! Grab a hold on this!'

While the officer had been bellowing so rudely at her, one of the other men, a big burly one, had been swinging a coil of rope, and he let it go.

Chastity watched it fly towards her, wondering if she'd be able to summon the energy to catch it, let alone swim to it if it missed by too much.

She needn't have worried, though, because it hit her squarely on the top of her head.

'Mind my bloody lenses, you oaf!' Chastity muttered and reached up to feel at the incredibly expensive lenses Freddy had bought her, worried that they might have been cracked.

It was only when the rope started slipping off her shoulder that she realised how irrationally she was acting. She forgot all about her lenses and grabbed for it, but her hands were too numb to grasp it, so she used most of her remaining strength to twirl her arm, wrapping the rope around it.

Her arm was almost wrenched from its socket as the men immediately began to haul her in.

She coughed and spluttered as the thin life jacket she'd been provided with proved incapable of keeping her head above the water and she briefly wondered what happened to pilots who bailed out over rougher seas.

In a surprisingly short time she was being hauled onto the cold metal of the undersea boat.

'Come on! Get her in!'

Chastity's legs were just as useless as her hands and she could do nothing to help them as they manhandled her through the hatch and passed her down into the waiting arms of a second group of sailors.

'Get that bloody hatch sealed! Prepare to dive!'

A man, standing in the centre of the room into which Chastity had been lowered, shouted at the sailors angrily and they carried her to one side and lowered her to the deck next to the wall before hurrying away to their duties.

Chastity lay there, conscious that she didn't exactly present the most dignified of pictures for an officer in the RAC, but completely unable to do anything about it; none of her limbs seemed to want to obey the orders she was giving them, apart from a few useless flopping motions. She immediately stopped trying to move entirely, not wanting to give more of an impression of a beached and dying fish than she already was - shivering uncontrollably, with her teeth chattering, dressed in white from head to toe and dripping sea water on the deck.

The warmth in the tin can was slowly seeping into her, though, making her drowsy. Her eyes began to close by themselves and she was only vaguely aware of the frantic activity going on around her. She barely noticed when the deck tilting alarmingly below her and the captain's continued shouted orders were only a dull booming in her ears as if she were hearing them under water. She hardly registered it when two female faces suddenly appeared in her vision, nor did she really feel it when they picked her up off the floor and dragged her out of the room, down a short adjoining corridor and into another room. Her flightsuit being stripped off brought her some way back to consciousness, though; despite the immodesty of the Misfit Squadron changing arrangements she still wasn't quite used to being unclothed around other people. However, it wasn't until a warm blanket had been wrapped around her and a hot cup of tea had been pressed into her hands that she truly started returning to full consciousness.

'Ah! There you are!' One of the women squatted in front of her and flashed a tiny light into her eyes. She was small, of obvious Indian ethnicity, with grey hair pulled back severely into a bun. There was a golden twin helix on her dark blue uniform jumper marking her as a full doctor and not just a combat medic. 'I'm Doctor Vaidya. How are you feeling?'

The woman's accent was quite thick and it took Chastity a moment to realise what she was being asked. 'Better. Thank you.'

'Very good, very good.' The light went off and the doctor placed it into her breast pocket, taking out a thermometer in its place and putting it in Chastity's mouth. While she waited for the mercury to expand, she grabbed her patient's wrist and looked at a watch on her own.

The second, much younger, woman, with the white helices of a nurse, was hovering in the background, holding some clothes, but when Chastity glanced up at her she blushed and looked away.

'Oh, that's very good.' The thermometer disappeared back where it came from and the doctor stood up. 'Let us get you dressed.'

The nurse stepped forward with the pile of clothes and shyly held them out.

'Thank you,' said Chastity as she took them, earning herself a nervous giggle in reply, before the young woman turned away and busied herself tidying up.

The doctor rolled her eyes. 'Ignore Janet, she is just a bit in awe of you.'

'Oh.' Chastity looked at the young woman, who blushed when she noticed the attention she was getting. 'She really doesn't have to be. I'm just a pilot.'

'But you are not just any pilot, are you?' The doctor gestured towards Chastity's white flightsuit, which was draped over a chair nearby, still dripping, and the Misfit Squadron patch on the front, opposite her wings.

There wasn't much Chastity could say, so she stood, took off the softly ticking heated blanket, and began to dress in the clothing - a set of, thankfully new, underwear, a pair of thick woollen socks, some plimsolls and dark blue coveralls with *HMS Udaipur* embroidered on the breast pocket.

When she was done, the doctor looked her up and down then nodded. 'Good. I think you are now well enough to see the captain. Come on!'

Without waiting for a reply or an acknowledgement, the Indian woman walked out through the oval doorway.

After a nod of thanks to the nurse, Janet, Chastity followed.

She had never been on an undersea boat before and she looked around with interest as the doctor led her back the way the two women had carried her.

Just about everything was metal: the hexagonal mesh floor; the walls; the doors; and the multitude of steel and brass pipes passing barely a foot over her head. It was actually very much like being on the inside of a proper ship, except, against her expectations, it seemed drier and smelled less damp. It was far from plain and purely serviceable, like the Arturo, though; it was more like something out of a Verne novel - the exposed surfaces of the pipes were covered in scrollwork and there were engravings covering every flat surface which showed men and women and even, bizarrely, elephants, with multiple heads or arms, all surrounded by leaves and flowers. It wasn't overwhelming, though, it was all done quite subtly and, despite the fantastical subject matter, tastefully.

The doctor led Chastity back to the room where she'd been brought aboard, which she supposed was the bridge, but stopped her just inside the door and gave her a look, warning her to keep quiet.

In sharp contrast to how it had been when she'd arrived, the room was silent, the atmosphere strained. The men and women scattered around the room were still and silent, staring at gauges, or standing ready at the myriad of wheels and levers covering the walls, ready to respond to an order at a moment's notice. The captain was leaning over a pair of women wearing headsets, with his hands on the backs of their chairs, watching them twiddling dials on something that looked like a radio.

'Anything?' he asked them in a voice barely above a whisper.

Both women shook their heads and the captain smiled and slapped the backs of their chairs. 'Looks like we got away with it, then!' He looked towards a woman standing against the wall to one side. 'Stand us down, Lieutenant.'

'Aye aye, sir.' She looked around. 'Stand down from general quarters.'

There was a collective sigh of relief and the tension flowed from the room. Shoulders relaxed, smiles broke out on faces and fully half of the men and women started drifting away, going through the doors at either end of the room and down the adjoining corridors.

The captain turned and took a step towards the table in the middle of the room, where charts were spread out, but when he caught sight of Chastity and the doctor his smile widened and he changed course towards them.

'Thank you, Doc.' The captain nodded at the Indian woman, then looked at Chastity. 'Welcome aboard, I'm Lieutenant Commander Anders, the captain of the Udaipur, and you are?'

Chastity drew herself up to attention, her old military habits asserting themselves once more, now she was far from the corrupting influence of her squadron. 'Aerial Officer Arrowsmith, sir.'

'At ease, Aerial Officer,' he smiled. 'You're one of the Misfits, I presume?'

'Yes, sir.'

'Good show, good show. Anyway, it's good to see you on your feet. We saw you go down, but we couldn't come up to get you until we were sure the last of the enemy aircraft were gone. Sorry we had to leave you in the drink for so long.'

'All's well that ends well, sir.' Chastity shrugged. 'When do we make port?'

'I'm afraid we're not going straight back to Malta.'

'But I need to get back to my squadron right away!'

Anders shook his head. 'That's not going to be impossible.'

'But...'

'Come over here.' The captain cut her off. He took her to the chart table and pulled a map of the sea between Malta and Sicily towards him. It was covered with contour lines showing the depth of the water and coloured arrows denoting what she assumed were currents. He pointed to a spot on it. 'My orders are to be here,' he pointed to another spot, some miles from the first, 'but we're here, because I stayed around to pick you up. We're on steams right now, when we shouldn't be, and we're going to be hard enough pressed to get on station as it is, without making the twenty-odd mile trip to Malta to drop you off first.'

'Can't you put me on one of the launches? Or a fishing boat?'

'I'm not going to risk this crew again by surfacing another time.'

'But there's nothing up there, you said it yourself.'

'I was wrong. We received a signal right after you came on board - Glidewing troops just got dropped on Gozo. So there *is* something up there - that big *Bertha* thing - and that means you're stuck with us until after the battle.'

The revelation that the Crimson Barons' airship was somewhere overhead and had managed to sneak Prussian troops onto the Maltese archipelago was devastating, but it was immediatcly overshadowed by the captain's last word. 'Battle?' Her voice came out squeakier than she intended and she found her lips were suddenly dry.

Anders nodded. 'There's an enemy fleet sailing for Malta. They left Catania about half an hour ago and should be about here by now.' He circled an area on the map, a quarter of the way from Sicily. 'That's why it's so important we get on station - we're supposed to be part of a line across the advance of the fleet which will close up around them just as you Wreckers attack in an hour from now.'

Chastity stared at the map. She didn't particularly like the idea of being in the undersea boat for any length of time; there was just something about being stuck in the depths of the ocean in a cramped and all too fragile tin can which terrified her, but the idea of being in it while explosions were going off all around...

'I... I...' Her vision narrowed until all that she could see was the small pencil cross with which the captain had marked his assigned position.

She swayed as her legs threatened to give way beneath her, but strong hands grabbed her before she could fall.

'Officer Arrowsmith!'

'Yes?' Captain Anders's concerned face loomed in front of her and she blinked and looked around, suddenly unsure where she was. 'What...?' Her head swam as everything came back to her in a rush and feelings of panic and claustrophobia threatened to overwhelm her once more, but this time she was ready for them and she clutched at the cold metal of the chart table as she took a few deep breaths.

I must not fear...

Her mother had scoffed at most of her father's spiritual beliefs and practises, but she had never stood in the way of him trying to teaching them to Chastity. She had never been particularly receptive, though, and had rejected most of his teachings, but for some reason the mantra to deal with fear had stuck. She'd never had cause to use it before, though, not even before her first time in combat, and she was actuality quite surprised when it worked.

After only a few seconds she was in control of herself enough to force a smile. 'I'm alright, thank you, sir.'

He returned her smile, tactfully not saying anything about her panic attack, then glanced at the doctor, who was hovering within arm's reach. 'Take her forward and get her a berth, please, Doc. And make sure she knows to stay there.'

'Aye aye, Captain.'

'Officer Arrowsmith.' Anders nodded at Chastity, then moved away to see to his duties.

Chastity had no way of knowing which way was forward or back in the boat, having no reference, so it was just as well the doctor was there to guide her. It turned out that the sick bay was forwards of the bridge and the crew quarters were just beyond that, although to call them "quarters" was a bit of an overstatement - the sleeping area for the crew was literally just five or six triple stacks of bunks on either side of the corridor that Chastity assumed went the length of the boat. The bunks for females were on one side, males on the other, although they were so close to each other that she didn't know why they bothered with the segregation.

There were twenty or so men and women in the moderately-sized space. Several were getting changed, putting on coveralls like her own, half a dozen were already snoring behind the curtains which pulled across the bunks for privacy, a few were lying on their beds, reading or writing, and five more were playing cards around one of the two small tables on either side of the aisle at the far end. She was moderately surprised to see that almost half of them seemed to be from the Indian subcontinent, like the doctor; she'd thought that the vast majority of the troops from that end of the Kingdom, like the Indians, the Australians and the New Zealanders, had been deployed on the Asian front.

There was an empty bunk about half way down and the doctor pointed to it. 'Here you are. Get some rest.' She smiled. 'Doctor's orders.'

'Thank you.'

The men and women had all stopped what they were doing to watch as the doctor walked her up the aisle between the beds and one of the men playing cards called out, just as Chastity was about to sit down.

'Who's this, Doc? Is this the pilot we just risked our lives to pick up?'

The man was in his mid-forties, grizzled, with greying black hair and a full beard. There was a sour expression on his face, which she suspected was permanent, and when Chastity met his eyes he glared at her hostilely.

There was a moment of stunned silence and the doctor bristled angrily, but before she could say anything, one of the two Indian youths at the table slapped the man on the arm with the back of his hand.

'Shut up, Pete! That's not just *any* pilot, that's *Chastity bloody Arrowsmith*, that is! She's the *best* of the Misfits!'

'Don't be chuffin' daft, Sanjay!' the other young Indian at the table chimed in. 'Abby Lennox is *obviously* the best!'

'Nah, Adi! Arrowsmith got more than twenty kills during the Battle over Britain, in a flippin' Spitsteam! Lennox got more, granted, but she had Dragonfly to do it in! Arrowsmith's the bee's knees, she is!'

Chastity wasn't sure which was more bizarre - the cockney accents coming out of the mouths of the Indian youths (*Chasti-ee blady Arasmiff!*) or the fact that they were debating her merits as a pilot in front of her as if she weren't even there.

She exchanged a glance with the doctor, who shrugged. 'I'll leave you to it. As I said, get some rest...' She gave the group around the table a scathing look - the debate had spread to the nearby beds as well and there were now almost a dozen people talking at once, everyone at that end of the room except the sour man, in fact. She shook her head. 'If you can.' She wandered away, still shaking her head.

None of the people discussing her were paying her a blind bit of notice, so Chastity sat on the bed, intending to obey the doctor's order. Her hand was on the curtain, ready to pull it across, but she stopped when she realised that the man on the bunk opposite, who'd been scribbling in a notebook, was looking at her.

'Um. Hello.'

'Chastity Arrowsmith, I presume?'

'How did you guess?'

She grinned and he smiled back at her. He was an intense-looking man with a very thin moustache on his upper lip, something she didn't think was permitted under Navy regulations.

'Eric Blair.'

'Pleased to meet you.' Chastity nodded in greeting, but then looked up and cringed as a creak of stressed metal rang out just about her head. 'I don't know how you can stand being shut up in tin can for hours on end. Especially during a battle.'

Blair shook his head. 'I can't. I hate it.'

Chastity frowned at him. 'Then why did you chose to be on an undersea boat?'

'I didn't. I work for the KBC - I'm here for research purposes.'

'You're writing an article?' Chastity pointed at the notebook in his lap.

'Not exactly.' He swivelled around so that he was sitting on the edge of the bunk and looked up and down the aisle, making sure that nobody was listening to them. 'The Prussians have been spreading propaganda throughout the subcontinent, telling the people there that King George is just using them for his own purposes and such. This boat was constructed and outfitted in India. Most of its crew came from there and every time it gets replacements they're usually more Indians, like Sanjay and Aditya there - they're Londoners, born and bred.' He gestured in the direction of the group at the end of the room, who were still arguing about her. 'So, rather than going half way around the world to India to judge the mood and look for ways of countering the Prussian efforts, I hopped on board last time the Udaipur was in

Gibraltar.' He gave her a wry smile. 'I haven't been able to come up with anything. I don't suppose you have any suggestions?'

Chastity shook her head. 'Sorry, I'm just a pilot.'

He chuckled as she echoed Sanjay's words. 'Come on, I've spoken to my fair share of pilots and I know that most of you have at least a *bit* of a brain on your shoulders. I also know that you Misfits are a damn sight smarter and worldly-wise than most. Just give me your opinion - it doesn't even have to be a particularly informed one.'

'Don't worry, it won't be.' Chastity grinned. She turned her head to watch the two Indian youths leading the discussion while she organised her thoughts. Despite their atrocious accents they were articulate and they seemed to be in the best of spirits. 'India has been the jewel in the British crown since Empress Victoria's time and Britain has always treated her very well - letting her govern herself and setting up universities and other public institutions, for example. Those of her citizens who wanted to come to England have been welcomed and, by the looks of things, have integrated well, while those who remain in India reportedly enjoy a vastly better standard of living than they were traditionally used to.' She shrugged. 'There are *always* going to be discontented people or lovers of chaos looking for an excuse to start trouble, but that's as true for Britain as it is for India and I don't think the Prussians are going to be any more successful there than they have been in Britain.'

'Neither do I,' he pulled a folded sheet of paper out of his notebook and handed it to her. 'But that hasn't stopped them trying. And if they're going to persist, then so must we.'

Chastity unfolded the paper. It was a typical Prussian propaganda leaflet, written in the usual Gothic script. However, where they usually decried the corruption of George VI or parliament and called upon the British working classes to rebel, this one appealed to the "downtrodden men and women of India".

She handed it back. 'If this hasn't worked in Britain, why would anyone think it would work in India?'

Blair again glanced around, betraying a paranoia that Chastity hadn't encountered in anyone else before, and his voice dropped so low that Chastity had to lean across the aisle to hear him. 'The KBC were actually ordered to send me out here by the Ministry of War. The Minister is worried that the people of the subcontinent won't be quite as stubborn or stiff-upper-lip-ish as the British were last summer and will give up at the first sign of an incursion by the Prussians or their allies.'

'*Is* there going to be an incursion?'

'If this war goes on much longer, then, with Japanese neutrality and that bloody pact between the Chinese and Kaiser Billy, I'd say it was inevitable. And if Malta...'

Blair was about to say more, but at that moment the people at the end of the room all stood and trooped down towards them. He watched them for a moment, then gave Chastity a sympathetic look before swinging his legs back onto his bed and jerking his curtains closed, leaving her to face the incoming assault alone.

The ten of them perched on the bunks around her and looked at her expectantly.

Rather surprisingly, it was the sour man, "Pete", who first spoke, though. 'Sorry, luv, didn't know who you were and what a good job you've been doing.' His voice was low, not much more than a grunt, but he seemed sincere. 'Me mates have put me straight. Hope there's no hard feelings.'

Chastity shook her head, but, before she could reply, the bombardment of questions began.

Thankfully, the sailors didn't pester her for too long. They got the answers to their most pressing, but largely frivolous questions - how life was in Misfit Squadron, whether she had met the King, what Abby Lennox and Gwen Stone were like, and whether Gwen was really in a relationship with Kitty Wright - but then Sanjay reminded them that the doctor had told her to get some rest. They drifted off to their bunks or back to their card game and left her to lie down. Just before she closed the curtains, she caught sight of Blair peering around the end of his. He grinned at her before twitching them back into place.

The thick curtains shut out the light and a surprising amount of noise and Chastity fell asleep almost immediately, exhausted after being up before dawn for the day's fighting and then bring dunked in the water.

She was woken after what seemed like only an instant by the blaring of a klaxon. It only sounded twice, but that was enough to send everyone tumbling out of their bunks.

Chastity pulled her curtain back and called across to Blair, who was the only one not rushing from the room. 'What's happening?'

'The enemy.' The man said enigmatically.

'But the captain said it would be an hour before the enemy ships were in range.'

'It *has* been an hour. You've been snoring like a sailor.' He grinned. 'And I should know.'

They watched the men and women rush out, some going forward - she knew which way that was now - some going towards the back of the boat, but after only a few seconds they were all gone and it was just the two of them.

Chastity looked back to Blair. 'What happens now?'

'Now we wait. Quietly.'

Silence fell, apart from the occasional creaking of the undersea boat's metal plating. It was only then that Chastity realised that the deep rumble, which had previously been a constant companion, droning in the background of conversation, had gone.

'I can't hear the engines. Have we stopped?' She whispered, feeling that to speak in a normal voice would be to bring the enemy ships down upon them.

Blair said nothing, he just put his hand on the bulkhead next to him and motioned for her to do the same.

It took quite a few seconds, but eventually she detected a slight vibration under her palm.

'Electrics,' Blair whispered. 'They're a heck of a lot quieter than the steam engines.'

'Why don't they run on electrics all the time, then?'

'Because the boat can't go as fast like this and the batteries don't last very long. They only really use the electric engines when there's an enemy around who could hear the steams.'

Chastity's eyes went up to the pipe-covered roof before she knew what she was doing, earning herself a chuckle from Blair.

She grinned at him sheepishly. 'Sorry.'

'Don't be; it's a natural reaction. You wait until there's actually something up there - just about everybody on the crew looks upwards just like you did.'

Blair smiled, then picked up his notepad and resumed his writing.

Chastity waited a few seconds, but when nothing more was forthcoming from the man she stood and looked up and down the aisle. The short corridor leading past the sick bay to the bridge was dark and uninviting, and she already knew what was that way, so she wandered in the other direction towards the front of the boat. Beyond the small table, which was still covered with cards from the game, there was a doorway leading to a kitchen. It was deserted and the light was off, so there wasn't much for her to see so she so walked back. She stopped at her bunk and looked around, at a loss for something to do. It was frustrating, and not a little bit strange, that the boat was preparing to go into a fight and yet she not only couldn't help, but had absolutely nothing to do with herself. What she wouldn't give to be in a Spitsteam at that moment.

'Would you like a book? I've got a few here - it'll help take your mind off things.'

Chastity looked down at Blair. She thought for a second then sat down. 'What have you got?'

Blair pulled a few battered books out of the small cubbyhole at the back of the bunk and shuffled through them to show her. 'I've got *The Prince, The Trial, The Man Who Would Be Emperor*, and one of my...'

He stopped and they both looked up as a woman appeared from the rear of the ship and hurried up the aisle to them.

She bobbed her head respectfully at Chastity. 'Captain's complements, ma'am, and he requests your presence on the bridge.'

Chastity leapt off the bunk, narrowly missing hitting her head on the one above in her rush. She smiled down at Blair. 'Thank you. I'll take you up on the offer later, if I'm still here.'

Blair nodded and returned her smile.

As the woman led Chastity away she thought she heard Blair mutter a reply. She didn't stop to find out for certain, but it sounded suspiciously like "if *any* of us are here".

The situation on the bridge was even more tense than it had been before, if that was at all possible, but this time it was the kind of tension that was only caused by the expectation of imminent action and mortal danger. Everyone was at their posts, attentive to their jobs, but they were all sneaking glances in the direction of the captain, who was standing behind the man at the radio, holding one of the cups of a headset to an ear.

Anders looked up when the woman brought Chastity in. He didn't say anything, just put down the headset, then tapped the radio operator on the shoulder and pointed up. In response, the man flipped a couple of levers.

For a moment nothing happened and Chastity was about to ask what he wanted, but then a voice came out of the tannoy speakers in the corners of the room.

'Haven, this is Trafalgar Leader, we are ten minutes to target.'

It wasn't loud, but it was very clear and Chastity was pretty sure it belonged to the man who commanded one of the bomber squadrons at Luqa.

The response came immediately - Dorothy Campbell's voice equally recognisable. 'Roger, Trafalgar Leader. Haven to all Sticklebacks, prepare to attack on my mark.'

The radio fell silent temporarily, with only the faint hiss of static, and the captain signalled for Chastity to join him at the chart table, where the chart of the sea between Sicily and Malta was spread.

'If everyone's where they should be, there are eight undersea boats along this line, here.' He pointed to a series of crosses pencilled in across the direct route from the east coast of Sicily to Malta. 'We're on the easternmost end, here.' He tapped the cross on the far right of the line. 'Unfortunately, the enemy aren't heading for Valletta as we thought they would, but rather to Gozo, which means that they will intercept the line a bit further west than we were expecting.' He dragged a finger through the line of boats, between the second and third.

'So you're out of position.'

'Correct. If things stay as they are they're going to pass us out of range of our torpedoes. We've been given the order to relocate, but on electrics we'll never make it. So...'

'Five minutes to target.'

Anders waited a second to see if anything else was going to come from the speakers and when it didn't he continued. 'So, when the Nelsons arrive and start dropping fishes in the water, we'll use the confusion to switch to steams and race into position to add our own to the mix.'

'Won't that give away our position?'

'Yes, but hopefully the Prussians will have enough to worry about already and won't have a chance...'

'Trafalgar Leader, you have anti-aircraft fire incoming from Bertha.' A new and very urgent voice, Abby's, came over the general channel.

'I see it, Badger Leader, I...'

The voice of the man was cut off suddenly and Chastity paled; it could only mean one thing.

Now more and more voices came over the speakers as panicked pilots transmitted on the general frequency rather than their squadron comms and Chastity flinched as a couple of screams tested the limits of the speakers. She wasn't accustomed to hearing such fear from British pilots, but she could imagine the scene above as the huge airship poured fire down at the lumbering bombers - they would be sitting ducks and feeling just as helpless as she did in the undersea boat.

Thankfully, it wasn't long before Campbell's voice came back on, her controller status overriding the multitude of other calls. 'Haven to all aircraft, abort mission. Return to base. All Sticklebacks stand down.'

The nightmare wasn't going to end there, though, because the Nelsons now had to retrace their steps, but Anders went over and tapped the radio operator on the shoulder. 'That's enough.'

The man flipped a couple of switches and silence returned, but Chastity could still hear the echoes of the screams, could still picture only too well the death and destruction being wrought just above the waves.

A shocked silence filled the bridge and the men and women around the room shared glances, shocked and saddened expressions on all their faces. A few of them looked to Anders for instructions, but he was just standing motionless, with his hands on the back of the radio operator's seat and his head down.

'Sir! Signal with our number!'

The shout of the telegraphist, sitting next to the radio operator, broke the spell and reminded Anders that there was still a job to be done, despite the tragic events in the sky. She scribbled furiously on a piece of paper as the signal, in Morse code, came in.

When she finished she tore it off her pad and held it over her shoulder for Anders, who grabbed it and read it quickly before calling out orders. 'Set course two zero zero, all ahead full.'

'Two zero zero, all ahead full, aye.'

Chastity almost fell onto the chart table as the boat turned sharper than she'd expected would have been possible before settling on its new heading.

'Lieutenant, you have the bridge.' The captain nodded at a woman who was standing to one side of the bridge, observing everything, then looked at Chastity. 'Come with me.'

He led her off the bridge towards the back of the boat and into a room just off the adjoining corridor. It was slightly smaller than the sick bay and, like it, a lot wider than it was deep. It was extremely cramped, containing a cot, a tiny table and a chair, with barely any room in between. He closed the door behind them, then waved her to the chair while he perched on the edge of the bed.

'The enemy are now only a couple of hours from Malta. We've been ordered to shadow them and prepare for another attack closer to the island.'

He hesitated and when he continued his voice was very low. 'What did we just hear? Was it as bad as it sounded? *Will* there be another attack from the RAC after that?'

Chastity grimaced. 'What we just heard was far too similar to what I saw and heard far too many times in France because we were going up against MU9's and 10's in machines that belonged in the First Great War. There, we lost at least half our aircraft every time we tried to do anything and I wouldn't be surprised if the same thing hadn't just happened.' She paused and looked him hard in the eye. 'Do not underestimate the RAC, though. If they say they will carry out another attack, they will.'

Anders met her gaze for a long second, then nodded, apparently satisfied. 'Good. Because we need them to provide some noise, otherwise we're going to lose most if not all of our boats when we attack. Because *whatever* the RAC do, we *will* be attacking.'

Chastity nodded earnestly. 'They'll play their part and it should be easier for them to get in range of the ships when they get closer to Malta. That airship won't be able to approach Malta close enough to make a difference because of the ack-ack coverage, so it'll just be down to the Fleas to stop the Nelsons.' She smiled wryly. 'And our fighters can deal with them a heck of a lot better than they can Bertha.'

'I hope so, because if we lose Malta then we lose a hell of a lot more than just a tiny island.'

'We're quite aware of that, Captain, and we'll fight just as hard as we did last summer.'

Anders nodded, then stood and went to open the door. 'I'll send someone to get you when the attack's about to begin. For now, I suggest you go back to your bunk and get some rest, so you can get back in the air as soon as we drop you off.'

'Aye aye, Captain.' Chastity grinned.

The mention of getting back in the air reminded her that she had left a very expensive flightsuit and set of lenses in sick bay. The suit was already starting to look a bit shabby - white hadn't been the best choice of colour for a combat flightsuit, but Freddy had insisted - and being soaked in salt water wouldn't do it any favours. She found that the nurse, Janet, had taken care of it, though. The suit, boots, gloves and helmet had all been rinsed and were now hanging in a kind of airing cupboard which was part of the ventilation system, along with her underwear and the boat's washing. With everything in hand as best as it could be, there was nothing she could do except thank Janet, who blushed shyly, then return to her bunk, so as not to be in the way in the tiny sick bay.

She was greeted by smiles and nods by the men and women in the bunk room, but they didn't pester her this time. The curtain was pulled across Blair's bunk so she just lay down on her own bed. Sleep wouldn't come, though, and after only a few minutes she sat up again and looked around. Half a dozen men and women were sitting around the table at the end of the room, munching on sandwiches and drinking tea. Her stomach rumbled at the sight and she suddenly realised that she was actually quite hungry so she stood and made her down the aisle towards them.

The Indian youth, Sanjay, looked up as she approached and smiled. 'There's tea and sarnies in the galley if you want 'em, luv.'

'Thank you.'

She went through the door into the kitchen, where three cooks were working to prepare the crew's lunch. They didn't look up as she came in and she didn't disturb them, she just filled a tin mug from the tea urn then piled some sandwiches on a plate.

The two round tables at the end of the bunk room had semi-circular benches around them and the men and women shifted up to make room for her. She nodded her thanks, then sat down and started to tuck in.

It didn't take long for her to notice that the sailors were all watching her while they ate and she looked around them and grinned. 'Do I have sauce on my face or something?'

There were a few chuckles, but they died out quickly as the sailors shared meaningful glances and subtle gestures, as if egging each other on. It was Sanjay who finally leaned forwards and spoke softly. 'Do you, uh, mind if we ask you something?'

'Of course not.'

'It's about the bombing that's going on in London... Well, you see, we've read what's in the papers, but it's always stuff about how people aren't giving up and that the British spirit is winning out. And that's all well and good, don't get me wrong, but we've heard rumours...'

He hesitated and the other youth, Adi, filled the gap. 'Yeah, we've heard rumours that the bombs are still falling and it's actually really bad.'

Sanjay nodded, picking up the reins again. 'That's right. And, well, none of us've been home in a year, so we haven't had a chance to see for ourselves what's really happening and we was hoping...'

Adi again chimed in when his friend paused. 'We was hoping you'd tell us what it's *really* like back home. You see, some of us are from London, we've got family there, and we haven't heard from them in a while...'

When Adi tailed off, nobody stepped up to continue, they just looked at her expectantly.

Chastity gazed around the group. When they had been asking her questions about the Misfits earlier they had been all smiles, joking and laughing at the comments being flung around, but now they were deadly serious and there were more than a few heads poking out from the bunks as well, listening intently.

She grimaced inwardly and sipped at her tea to buy time to sort out her thoughts. She wasn't sure it should be her talking to these people, but she was all they had and she wasn't going to just brush them off. However, she wasn't sure she was going to be able to provide them with the answers they needed.

'I was in central London over Midwinter, before I shipped out to Malta, and it's almost untouched. There's some random bomb damage, but nothing substantial, and people are shopping and walking down the street as they always have. It was the East End that got hit the worst, though. I haven't been there myself, I can only tell you what I've seen from the air and have heard from people who've been there.' She paused and looked at Sanjay and Adi, knowing from their accents that they would be more worried by what she had to say next. 'Over the summer, on days without much wind, you could see the smoke of the fires in the East End rising into the air from Biggin Hill, where I was posted. During the day the Prussians pounded it with everything they had, aiming for the factories and the docks, I suppose, but more often than not hitting the houses. Then, at night, they came back and used the fires they'd started to guide them. One of my mates, Roberta Collingwood,' Chastity faltered and had to cough to clear the lump in her throat, which still arose whenever she thought of her friend, before she could continue, 'she was from Stepney. She went back to see her folks on her day off, I think it was the ninth or tenth of September.

She told me that when she came out of Stepney Green station she had to ask for directions to her house - she'd lived there all her life and she had to ask for directions because she wasn't sure she was in the right place!'

She saw the faces around her fall, as the men and women took in what she was telling them and most likely imagined what would have to happen for them not to no longer be able to recognise the town, village, or neighbourhood that they had grown up in. She didn't really need to go on; that image would probably be enough for them, but she did - the destruction wasn't the whole story and they needed to know the rest.

'What they write in the press is true, though. The people aren't letting the destruction stop them and they're keeping their spirits up and contributing to the fight as best they can. They're not even in very much danger, with the amount of public air raid shelters the King built. They're even using the underground stations if they have to. So, if you're not getting letters from home, it doesn't necessarily mean the worst; there are plenty of reasons mail won't be getting through to Malta.'

Even though they weren't particularly happy about what Chastity had said, the sailors seemed to accept her words, but nobody said anything more while they finished their snacks. They drifted away one by one to their bunks until it was only Chastity left. She polished off the last of her sandwiches, washed it down with the dregs of her tea, then took the mug and plate into the galley before making her way to her own bunk to wait for the attack to begin. She found a book on her pillow, "Burmese Nights", by an author she didn't know - George Orwell, and she looked over at Blair's bunk, but his curtain was still drawn so she lay down and opened the book.

She quickly lost herself in the tale of intrigue set in the twenties in Burma, when anybody who was anybody had spent at least a season seeing and being seen in one of the richest and most opulent countries of the British Empire. About ten minutes after she started, the vibration through the metal of the boat increased when it switched from electrics to steam and she stopped reading and looked around. However, when nobody else seemed to think anything untoward was happening she returned to the book without seeking an explanation. It wasn't until the boat went back on electrics some time later and the klaxon sounded, ordering everyone to quarters, that she finally closed it and sat up to watch the sailors racing to their posts.

Blair's curtain was pulled back - she had been so engrossed in the story that she hadn't noticed him do it - and when the noise had abated, the last of the sailors disappearing from the room, he nodded at the book. 'You're enjoying it, then?'

'I am! Thank you. I'm going to have to find some of the other books from this author.'

'He's not bad, is he?' He seemed about to say something else, but was prevented from doing so when a man rushed down the corridor towards them and instead just gave her a wry smile. 'Looks like the captain's summoning you to witness the battle again.'

Blair was correct and Chastity followed the man to the bridge where the captain greeted her.

'Aerial Officer, just in time. The attack's about to begin.' He motioned for her to take a seat next to the radio operator and handed her a headset. 'You're going to have to listen to things on those, I'm afraid; I don't usually put what's happening on the tannoy and after what happened last time I probably won't ever again. He patted the back of the radio operator's chair. 'If anything untoward happens, stick with Geoff here, he'll let you know what you have to do.' He turned away, but then stopped as something occurred to him. 'Oh, and when this is all over you can tell me what the hell "meltbombs" are.'

'Will do, sir.' Chastity grinned.

She smiled at the radio operator, Geoff, then sat and put the headset on. She was immediately surrounded by the voices of her friends, laughing and joking as they always did before a fight. She grinned; the Misfits were transmitting their banter over the general frequency, which was a gross contravention of radio discipline and precisely the kind of thing Abby or Dot or both would do to bolster the morale of the other RAC pilots.

The Misfits had apparently been sent in first to create a bit of chaos before the more vulnerable Nelson's made their run and she listened as they celebrated hit after hit with the weapons that Wendy Llewellyn had cooked up - the meltbombs that Anders had mentioned.

After a couple of frantic minutes, a new voice, calmer and far more businesslike than the Misfit ones, came on. 'Badger Leader, this is Trafalgar Leader, we are one minute out.'

Abby didn't rein back her enthusiasm one bit in reply, though and Chastity smiled at her reply. 'Roger, Trafalgar Leader. Badgers, time to give that battleship something to think about.'

No sooner had the leader of the Nelsons reported in, then Captain Anders began shooting orders around the bridge and Chastity slipped an ear out of the headset so she could listen to him as well.

A wave of excitement and anticipation ran through the men and women on the bridge as the undersea boat surged forwards to rapidly close the gap with the enemy fleet. At the same time the deck tilted as it rose up through the water and there were several thunks that Chastity felt through the thin soles of her shoes as torpedoes were loaded.

The captain moved to the periscope, mounted on a thin column near the chart table, and peered through the eyepieces. A series of orders from him brought forth all sorts of numbers from the men and women around the room. Chastity had no idea what most of the numbers meant, but they apparently satisfied Anders and four torpedoes were sent on their way in rapid succession.

'Incoming fire! Twelve o'clock high!' The deck tilted as the undersea boat dived again and Chastity turned her attention back to the headset just in time to hear the panicked call from the leader of the Nelson squadrons. For a moment she wondered what had spooked him, but Gwen's reply told her all she needed to know - Bertha was back.

'What in Shakespeare's name is that thing doing here? Doesn't Gruber know they're in range of our guns?'

'I'm sure he does, but unless he's on board I'm not su...' Drake's voice faded suddenly and was replaced by static.

Chastity turned to ask the radio operator why he wasn't moving to fix the problem, but he forestalled her, shaking his head. 'We've gone too deep, the signal won't reach.'

Chastity frowned. One of the few things she knew about undersea boat warfare was that torpedoes had to be fired close to the surface if you wanted to have a chance of hitting a ship. 'Why would we...'

'Charges in the water!'

Before Chastity could ask what a charge was, a huge explosion shook the boat, throwing her out of her seat and to her hands and knees on the floor. The rest of the crew were able to keep their feet, having grabbed onto whatever they could as soon as the shout had gone out.

Just as she was picking herself up, the boat was rocked by another explosion, knocking her over again. She hit her head on the support of her chair and fell to the deck, stunned.

'Stay down, Arrowsmith!' The captain shouted at her exasperatedly, in between roaring orders at his crew.

Another couple of explosions came, even louder and stronger than the first ones and Chastity cried out and wrapped her arms around her head as the boat shook and its metal complained. She screamed when a torrent of freezing cold water hit her and tried to roll out of the way, but between the chair and the chart table there was nowhere for her to go.

Hands grabbed her under the armpits and dragged her out of the way so that men and women could rush to stop the leak or whatever it was.

The soaking served to rouse her somewhat and spur her into action and she rolled over and grabbed at the edge of the chart table and used it to pull herself up. Another deafening explosion went off just as she got to her feet and the boat rolled nauseatingly, but this time she managed to hold on. The lights flickered and another leak started in the corridor outside sick bay, sending a repair crew rushing for it.

Chastity squeezed her eyes shut, waiting for the next explosion, for the one that would open the boat like a can of sardines and send dark water rushing in. She flinched as the boat was buffeted again, but the noise was duller, the impact less. The next one didn't even cause the boat to tremble - the storm was moving off.

She took a deep breath, then forced herself to open her eyes. She was shaking, her heart pounding in her ears almost as loud as the explosions had, but when she looked around the bridge she found that everyone else was calmly at their posts, as if nothing had happened, as if they hadn't been only feet, or perhaps even mere inches, from death.

'Enemy ship is moving away, Captain.'

'Take us up to firing depth!'

Chastity blinked at Anders. Instead of slinking away to lick his wounds, like she'd thought he would, he was not only taking them back into the fight, but barely waiting for the ship that had been hunting them to go away.

The deck tilted sharply and she pressed her lips together tightly to stop herself from showing how terrified she was when the boat creaked alarmingly with the change in pressure. She nervously eyed the places where water had come in before, but to her relief there was no sign that the stress of the climb was going to reopen the wounds.

The boat levelled off before long and the captain hurriedly raised the periscope. He made an extremely quick and almost comical shuffling circuit of the pillar to look all around the boat, before settling on a target. He went through the same series of commands in quick succession then fired torpedoes, but instead of immediately diving he beckoned to Chastity.

'Come take a look.'

Chastity released her death grip on the edge of the chart table and walked stiffly over to the periscope. She flexed her aching fingers then took hold of the handles and pulled the eyepiece of the periscope down to her height before leaning into it.

The scene was almost apocalyptic, the horizon filled with blocky grey shapes from which red and black smoke streamed into the sky. Considering the attack had only just begun, the results were impressive and extensive.

'I take it the red smoke is something to do with those meltbombs?'

Chastity tore her eyes away from the sight to look at the captain. 'Yes. Red marks a hit.'

Anders gave her a wry smile. 'If those things are at all effective, then there's almost no need for any of us to do anything more; just about every ship in their fleet has been hit.'

Chastity nodded enthusiastically. 'Oh, yes, they're very effective. We've found that a couple of hits are usually enough to sink even the largest of ships.'

'Just as well, because we're out of torpedoes and are going to have to retreat. May I?' Anders gestured at the periscope and Chastity reluctantly backed away.

Anders took one last look around, then flipped up the handles and brought down the periscope. 'Take us down. Set course one one zero.'

He looked at Chastity. 'There's nothing more we can do here, so we're going to lay a few miles off the coast until it's safe to dock at Manoel Island. By any luck you should be home by tea time!' He glanced at the clock on the wall. 'Why don't you get some lunch. I'll send a messenger when we know anything.'

Chastity knew when she was being dismissed, so she nodded and began to go.

'Oh, and visit the doc on your way, get her to see to your head.'

Chastity frowned and turned back. 'My head?' She put her hand up to her forehead and was shocked when it came back coated in blood. She'd thought the liquid on her face was water from the burst pipe, but it looked like she'd done herself a bit of a mischief tumbling out of her chair.

'Aye aye, sir!' She grinned and made her way out.

It turned out that Chastity had only a very shallow cut on her head, but such was the nature of head wounds that it was bleeding quite profusely. The doctor had her work cut out to stop it without shaving the hair surrounding it, but she eventually succeeded and sent Chastity on her way after putting a dressing on it.

When she got back to the bunk room, the off duty personnel were having lunch, but Chastity didn't feel particularly hungry, having gorged on sandwiches earlier. She much preferred to spend her time reading more of the book Blair had lent her anyway, hoping to finish it before they got to Malta and she had to give it back.

Blair was at the end of the room eating, so she just lay down, grabbed the book and took up from where she had left off.

Once again she lost herself in the story, but this time she was only permitted fifteen or twenty minutes to read before she was interrupted by a messenger asking her to go and see the captain.

Anders was in his stateroom, sitting hunched over on his bed, with his head in his hands and she was struck by how tired he looked, his eyes red with dark black bags underneath them and his skin with a greyish tinge to it. Her eyes went to the piece of paper on his lap, a message slip, and she wondered what news he could have received that had so sapped the life from him.

The door was open, but he hadn't noticed her arrival so she knocked on the door frame before announcing herself. 'You wanted to see me, Captain?'

He finally looked up, although it took a moment for him to focus on her. 'Ah, yes. Come in, Arrowsmith. Pull up a pew.' His voice had no energy in it and the hand he waved at the chair was almost limp.

He waited for her to sit down before waving the message. 'We've been ordered to retreat to Alexandria immediately.'

Chastity couldn't believe her ears. 'But the attack... I thought we'd all but destroyed their fleet!'

Anders shook his head. 'Apparently your meltbombs weren't quite as effective as we'd been made to believe and the only ships that were sunk were the ones hit by torpedoes, which was less than half of them. The troop ships are already offloading in Gozo and Valletta is being blockaded by the war ships, so we can't drop you off. You don't particularly want to be on Malta anyway, because the island is surrendering.'

Chastity just stared at him. There was nothing she could really say in the face of such devastating news. With the setbacks in Greece, Crete and now Malta, the British would more than likely lose all access to the Mediterranean, which meant that their interests in North Africa would be cut off and the troops starved of supplies. It wouldn't take long for Egypt to fall and the road east to India and Burma would be open for the Prussians and Italians - the dominoes would continue to fall one by one, and it wasn't as if the Kingdom of Britain had too many left to play as it was.

'Oh, and I'm sorry to say that we've been under radio silence since before you come on board and we've been ordered to remain that way until we reach Alexandria. So, I'm afraid we haven't been able to make arrangements for you to rendezvous with your squadron or even tell anybody we have you.'

Chastity went pale. 'So, everybody thinks I'm dead.'

'Probably, but we'll set them straight when we get to Egypt, don't you worry.' Anders looked at her thoughtfully. 'Is there someone who would be particularly upset if they thought you were dead? Someone on the island maybe?'

Chastity nodded. 'There is, but he's back in England. Hopefully, the news of my demise won't reach him before I do.'

'I sincerely hope so.' Anders took a deep breath. 'Well, that's all I wanted to say - we're done in Malta, for now anyway, and you're stuck with us for a bit longer than you'd hoped. Sorry.'

'That's alright, sir, there are worse places to be.'

'Yes there are,' Anders grinned, 'just wait till you see Alex.'

Chastity laughed. 'You'll have to show me the sights, then, sir.'

'I will.'

He gave her a nod and she returned it, then stood and made her way out.

It had all been smiles with Anders towards the end, but the true reality of her situation, and the situation of the war in general, hit her on the walk back to the bunk room and by the time she made it to her bed she was feeling thoroughly down in the dumps.

She sat heavily on her bed and stared at the floor as her mind raced

It would only be a few days before the boat arrived in Alexandria, but it would take her far longer to get back to the Misfits, or to England. She wasn't going to be able to take a ship back across the Mediterranean so she would have to find a berth on an undersea boat making the trip to Gibraltar or somehow get out across the land, although in which direction she could go she had no idea. And it wasn't as if she was going to be very high on the list for transport, either, nor would she expect to be; sick, wounded and civilians had to be evacuated first.

Her prospects for the immediate future didn't exactly look good.

She sighed and lay down, but then squirmed uncomfortably when something poked her in the back. She wriggled around and reached behind her to pull whatever it was out and looked at it.

'Oh well, Berty,' she thought, 'at least I'll have time to finish this book.'

LEFT BEHIND

LEFT BEHIND

Malta, May 1941

A noise woke Kitty and she opened her eyes with a start.

'Gwen? Is that you?' She struggled, trying to sit up, but her body refused to respond and she was only able to prop herself up on her elbows. The room was dark, the only light coming through a crack under the door, but she could just about make out a shadowy form sitting beside her and a wooden chair creaked as it moved.

A hand gently pressed her back down onto the bed 'There now, just relax.'

Kitty smiled at the soft voice. She should have known Gwen would be with her when she woke up.

'I had a horrible nightmare. Prussian assassins were chasing us around the house in Oxfordshire.'

'Well, you're safe and sound now, in the hospital on good old Malta.'

'Malta? What are we doing...?' Everything came back to Kitty in a rush and she swore; she would actually prefer confronting the assassins to still being stuck on the island, cut off from friendly forces and with dwindling supplies. 'Oh, bloody hell.' She tried to sit up again and groaned as pain shot through her whole body and dizziness threatened to overwhelm her. 'What happened? You said I was in the hospital? What's wrong with me?'

'You don't remember?'

'No. I...' Kitty frowned. 'I was shot down I think. Gruber...' She clutched at vague memories of red aircraft, but they were as elusive as the machines themselves.

'You were. And you were hurt badly. You've been asleep for two weeks.'

'Two weeks!' Kitty gasped and reached up to cup a soft cheek. While the time had passed in an instant for her, for Gwen it must have been an eternity of worry and constant fighting. 'Two weeks is *far* too long to go without a kiss, darling. How about it?'

There was a chuckle and the shadowy figure leaned down.

Kitty felt a moment of panic as she realised that she hadn't cleaned her teeth in a couple of weeks, but then soft lips were pressed against hers and all her concerns were banished. Her mouth opened involuntarily in a sigh as the kiss deepened, but then suddenly the contact was gone.

'Aw! What's wrong?' Kitty pouted and reached out to pull Gwen back, but the bed shifted as the woman stood and moved away.

'Gwen?'

There was the clicking of clockwork being wound and then a soft light bloomed from a lamp on the bedside table.

The first thing Kitty saw was that she was in a tiny room, seemingly hewed from rock. The second thing she saw was that it wasn't Gwen standing by her, but Polly Ames, the medical orderly that she and Gwen had befriended on the Arturo.

The pretty young woman had a sheepish look on her face and her cheeks were almost as dark as her freckles.

'Polly?'

'Sorry, Kitty, I just couldn't resist.'

Kitty laughed, but then groaned when her insides protested again. 'I'll forgive you this once.' She squeezed out the words with what little breath she could catch. 'Where's Gwen?'

'She's gone. She and the rest of the Misfits left the day you were shot down.'

'Gone?' Kitty blinked in confusion. There was no way it could be true; Gwen would never have abandoned her, she would have done whatever she'd had to in order to stay by her side, including, knowing her, deliberately getting herself arrested. 'She can't be gone.'

'She is. Sorry. *All* the British have gone from Malta.' Polly said in a soft voice. 'We lost and had to abandon the island.'

'No.' Kitty shook her head. 'That's not possible...'

For some reason the light was fading, as if the clockwork was winding down already, but strangely Polly's voice was also becoming quite indistinct, as if she were speaking underwater...

'Kitty? Kitty!'

Her eyes hurt from staring up into the sun, but she didn't dare look away; the red aircraft was up there somewhere. She was certain that the moment she looked away it would pounce and she needed to know the moment it did if she were to have any hope of surviving. Something was wrong with her aircraft, though, it felt sluggish around her, the controls not responding how they should to the commands her hands and feet were giving them.

She spared a moment to glance at her wings, checking the control surfaces for damage or obstructions. They seemed fine, but there was no denying that there was a heaviness to the stick and pedals.

She tilted her head back to resume her scan of the sky but, instead of the vast blue emptiness, she found Gruber's aircraft, Hölle, filling her vision, pinpricks of light winking from its wings.

Her body convulsed as metal tore through her and she jerked back and forth, flailing her limbs and screaming as the hot agony proved too much for her. The straps across her shoulders proved insufficient to keep her in place and they snapped, setting her free to roll and twist in her seat.

Hold her down!

The voice over the radio was unfamiliar, but it sparked something in her, some memory, and, as a warm liquid feeling flooded through her, she felt herself relax, her body losing all power to move. At the same time the pain dissipated, leaving her with just a buzzing in her ears that wasn't entirely unpleasant.

The sun still beat down upon her, bright through the ruined canopy, but she could no longer feel the heat of it, instead it was a cool, brilliant white and she blinked, more surprised than shocked as something came between her and it.

Suddenly, the spell was broken and she remembered.

'Polly?' The word came out as little more than a croak from her tortured vocal chords, but the woman bending over her understood.

'I'm here, Kitty, I'm here.'

'What...?'

'You had a seizure, but you're alright now, the doctors have got it under control.'

Polly moved and Kitty winced as the light returned, the overhead surgical lamp far too bright.

'Oops, sorry!' Polly reached up and tilted the light, diverting its beam away.

Another figure joined the young woman in her field of vision and another light shone into her eyes, but this one was far smaller and not nearly as bright.

'Hello, Kitty, I'm Doctor Brown. Do you know where you are?'

'Malta?'

'That's right, very good.' The light went off and Kitty found herself looking up at a young man wearing a surgical cap and mask. 'You had a bit of a turn. It happens sometimes when someone's on as many painkillers as you are, but I'm afraid you tore some of your stitches. I'm going to have to go in and sew you up again before you lose too much blood. That means you have to go under again, sorry.'

Kitty tried to reply, but her tongue was thick in her mouth and all she could manage was a moan.

The last thing she saw before the darkness reclaimed her was Polly standing beside her, tears streaming from red-rimmed eyes.

When Kitty woke up it was dark, with not even any light coming underneath the door.

'Polly?' It took her three attempts to get the word out and even then it was barely audible, but the silence surrounding her was so profound that the young woman would have heard had she been there.

There was no reply. She was on her own.

Thoughts of being mistaken for dead and the avant-garde production of Romeo and Juliet that had given her nightmares when she was five flashed through her mind. She tried to reach the clockwork lamp, to at least give herself the comfort of light, but found that she couldn't move. Her breathing sped up along with her heart and she felt a scream rising in her throat, but she forced it down with pure willpower and images of how her reunion with Gwen would be.

It was only when she had herself better under control that she noticed the tightness around her arms and legs and realised that she was strapped to the bed, probably to stop her hurting herself again. It was a wise precaution, but she just wished someone had been there to let her know they had done it before thoughts of paralysis and life as an invalid had put her into a spin.

Even though she had calmed down a bit and was no longer on the verge of panicking, her situation still wasn't exactly a pleasant one, so she continued with her daydreaming. She pictured the two of them in Gwen's airship, floating in supreme comfort across the Atlantic, directly to New York where they would disembark and spend a few weeks in style in one of the luxury hotels, in a room on at least the thirtieth floor with a view of the entire island, before taking to the skies again and flying to Ohio, to her family home, where she would introduce Gwen to her parents...

Her imaginings ran away with her and she slipped back into oblivion with a smile on her face.

'Miss Wright? Can you hear me? Miss Wright?'

'Unh...'

Kitty opened her eyes to light. It wasn't nearly as bright as previously, but it still hurt and she squeezed them shut again almost immediately.

'Open your eyes, please, Miss Wright.'

'Don't wanna.'

There was a chuckle from beside her left ear and Kitty turned her head and forced her eyes open.

Polly was there, perched on a stool by the bed. 'Let the doctor do his tests, there's a good girl.'

'OK, but only because you asked so nicely.' Kitty smiled at her, receiving a beaming grin in return, then looked at the doctor. 'Go ahead, do your worst, Doc.'

She was fairly sure it was the same doctor as before - his face had been hidden behind a mask in the surgery but she thought she recognised his eyes. He was surprisingly young, probably only a couple of years older than her, but his eyes were sunken with exhaustion and his forehead creased with worry lines, making him seem much older.

The young man prodded and poked her, enlisting Polly's help to roll her onto her sides and manipulate her leg, which Kitty refused to look at again after catching a single glimpse of what a mess it was. The whole process took only a few minutes and then the doctor wrote a few things on the clipboard hanging on the end of her bed, nodded to her and hurried out without saying another word.

Kitty looked at the young woman questioningly.

Polly shrugged. 'He's a good doctor, he's just a bit swamped at the moment.' She sat back down on the stool, then leaned over to brush an errant hair from Kitty's eyes. 'How are you feeling?'

'Like hell. What's wrong with me?'

'You got hit by two bullets, one in your side and one in your leg. Neither of them were immediately fatal, obviously, but you lost a lot of blood and passed out under your glidewings. You're lucky to be alive.' She grimaced. 'I'm afraid the medics on the launch that picked you up had to cut off your flightsuit, though. I have the pieces, but I don't think anything can be done with it, sorry.'

Kitty shrugged as best she could, feigning indifference. 'Doesn't matter; it's only a flightsuit.' It was a lie, though; her grandfather had given her that suit when he'd found out she was going to fight for freedom in Spain. It had been as much a part of her as Hawk and it felt like another piece of what made her herself had been ripped away.

She put the suit out of her mind and forced a smile. 'So, I'll get better soon, then?'

Polly nodded. 'The seizure set you back a bit, but it's just a matter of time before you're back on your feet again.'

'Good.' Kitty took a deep breath and winced as something pulled uncomfortably in her side.

Polly was instantly on her feet looking down at her in concern. 'Does something hurt? Shall I get the doctor back?'

Kitty shook her head. 'It's nothing, I just need to stop breathing so much.'

'Oh, alri... Hang on, what did you...?' Polly tutted and shook her head as Kitty grinned up at her. 'That's not funny.'

'It is from where I'm lying.' Kitty shook her head gently. 'Just sit down, I'll be fine. Tell me what I've missed. You said the island was evacuated the day I was shot down? Why? How did we lose?'

'I don't know the details, I just know that the Prussians dropped glidewing troops onto Gozo then sailed a fleet over from Sicily which we couldn't stop. There was no way to hold the island, so the Arturo was loaded up with everything and everyone, then sneaked away during the night.'

'And they just left us?'

'They had to; if we'd tried to move you, you would have died. Same for the other patents here. It's fairly safe, though; the hospital was collapsed above us so the enemy have no idea we're here. We're not trapped, though, because there's a secret tunnel which connects to the sea behind a hidden door, directly opposite the stairs on the fifth floor. We've been receiving supplies and moving patients off the island by undersea boat through there every few days since the island fell.'

'So it's not just me here?'

Polly shook her head. 'No. We had a sixty-two critically wounded people here initially. Thirteen have been evacuated since then, along with some of the support staff, leaving forty-nine, including you and eight doctors and nurses.'

'OK.' Kitty tried to nod, but she found that things were becoming a bit fuzzy once more, the room fading around her and her body somehow becoming more distant and beyond her control. 'I think I'm...'

'Kitty! Kitty!'

The soft but insistent voice brought her back to consciousness and to pain. She moaned as her eyes fluttered open and she became aware of the woman standing over her. 'Polly?' The word was slurred, almost unrecognisable in her own ears, her tongue thick and dry. 'Whas going on?'

'You have to wake up, you have to get moving.'

'Can't. Hurts.'

'You have to. The Prussians are coming.'

'No. Safe. Unnerground.'

'They're digging. Listen.'

Kitty did as she was told and gradually became aware of a scratching sound, punctuated by occasional knocks. It was probably her imagination, but it seemed to be getting louder, coming closer with every passing second, filling her head.

'They started this morning and we think they'll break through in an hour at the most.'

'Oh.' The information swam around in Kitty's head. She knew it was bad; the girl's distress told her that much, but try as she might she couldn't quite grasp what it meant, or work out what she should do about it.

'Ames, say goodbye and get out here! We need you!'

Polly spun around as an older woman called out to her from the doorway.

'Coming, ma'am!' Polly replied, but the woman had already gone.

She turned back to Kitty. 'There's an undersea boat here, but it'll be the last one and anyone not on it will be captured. The lieutenant refuses to risk moving you and the others on this floor, though; he says you're better off being left for the Prussians to take care of. You have to prove him wrong and get downstairs by yourself, but you must do it quickly; they're sealing the tunnels behind us in ten or fifteen minutes to slow the Prussians down.'

'I can't!'

'You have to!' Polly stood and took a reluctant step away. 'I'm sorry, Kitty.'

'Polly!' Kitty reached out to stop her, the reality of her situation finally breaking through the haze, but the young woman was gone, her running footsteps resounding in the corridor outside, and after only a few seconds even that had faded to nothing.

Kitty subsided back onto the bed with a moan.

It was impossible for her to do what Polly was asking of her; she was in too much pain to move, let alone walk, so she closed her eyes and resigned herself to being taken captive by the Prussians. According to Drake they had some wonderful medical technology and she would probably be back on her feet in a couple of days. Although, she didn't know what good that would do her if Gruber locked her up in Bertha. That was undoubtedly what would happen; Gruber had almost gotten his grubby mitts on her once before, he wouldn't let her escape him again and the Italians wouldn't be able to do anything to help her this time.

The pain was the worst it had been since she had been shot down. Her leg was killing her and it felt like someone was stabbing her repeatedly in the side. She peeled back the bedsheets and lifted her head to look down at her body, but then stopped when she realised what she had done. The muscles in her abdomen were all but useless, but she could lift both her arms. And her legs...

She almost blacked out from the pain when she tried to move her wounded leg, but after some careful trials the other one seemed to work more or less alright.

Renewed banging and scratching caught her attention. It was definitely louder now, it wasn't her imagination, and the thought of the ceiling caving in on her when the Prussians broke through and finishing the job that Hans Gruber had started finally spurred her into action.

She threw back the sheet, ripping it off the bed entirely so that it wouldn't tangle with her limbs, then rolled carefully onto her good side, gritting her teeth as her bad leg shifted and fire shot up through her hip. When it subsided enough for her to be able to think again, she slid her good leg out, putting it onto the floor, then used both her hands to lift and lower the other one. The pain in her abdomen was intense, her stomach muscles pulling at whatever was wrong inside her, but she eventually managed to get both feet flat on the floor and sit up properly.

She stayed there, panting for breath, as tracers flared behind her eyes and the world receded as if she were pulling high G forces.

She didn't know how long she sat there, but eventually she recovered just enough to move again.

Someone had left a pair of wooden crutches by the bed, long ones that went all the way up under the armpits and she grabbed them and manoeuvred them around in front of her. Getting up onto them wasn't hard, but once she was up, balance was a definite problem - if only having one good leg wasn't quite enough to tip her over, her head spinning at the effort certainly was and she crashed headfirst to the floor.

If she'd had any breath in her body she would have screamed as both her leg and side landed on one of the crutches. As it was she couldn't do anything except lie still as her short-circuited brain refused to give any commands to her body. She refused to let it subside into comfortable nothingness, though, knowing that if she did then she would never wake up in time to make it to the undersea boat.

She had fallen in such a position that the top half of her body was out of the room and she could see all the way down the corridor to the open door at the end and what looked like the stairwell beyond. While she was watching, a group of people hobbled by, heading down the stairs, shepherded by a couple of women in orderly uniforms. None of them looked in her direction and, like Polly, they were gone in moments, before she had a chance to cry for help.

She kept watching, gathering her forces to call out to whoever passed next, but after several long minutes nobody else had gone by and she began to worry that she'd be left behind.

'Come on, Kitty, you can do this.' *You* have *to do this.*

She had learned her lesson from her first aborted attempt to walk and this time she took things a lot more slowly. Judicial use of the door frame reduced the strain on her stomach muscle considerably and she managed to get up on the crutches again fairly easily and painlessly, then began her long trek down the short corridor.

She stopped again almost immediately when she came across two open doors, one on each side of the corridor. In one of the rooms a figure, wrapped from head to toe in bandages so she couldn't tell if it were a man or a woman, was lying motionless on a bed, while in the other a distinctly green looking woman was moaning softly in her sleep as she writhed gently.

There was nothing she could do for either of them - she was having enough trouble getting herself down the corridor without trying to drag anyone else - so she passed them by with only a sympathetic look, which of course went unnoticed.

She passed six more rooms before she reached the end of the corridor. Two held men who looked more dead than alive, connected up to breathing machines that wheezed and hissed softly, three were empty, but the last held a woman, who regarded her with sunken eyes as she crossed the doorway. She said nothing and Kitty didn't dare spare the time to stop to speak to her, but the slow speed she was making on the crutches afforded her ample opportunity to notice the dozens of tubes and wires connecting her to large machines surrounding her, effectively anchoring her to the room.

Kitty reached the end of the corridor, where it let out into the stairwell and stopped, wheezing for breath and unable to go any further. She leaned against the door jamb to rest and looked into the tubular space. As she'd expected, the lift in the centre of the stairway was dark and silent so she would have to take the stairs, but things weren't quite as bad as she'd feared; she had expected to be on the first floor in intensive care, giving her five flights of stairs to negotiate, but instead the number on the wall told her she was on the third floor. That was where the people who were no longer critical but still needed looking after day and night were moved to - it was where the Misfits had visited Owen after he'd been released from the burn ward.

Three flights of stairs were still far more than she felt like she could handle at that moment, though, with her body aching like it did and her head seemingly filled with cotton wool. All she wanted to do was slide down the wall, get herself comfortable, close her eyes and sleep until the Prussians broke through, which by the sound of things would be any moment.

The noise was increasing rapidly and she looked up, even though all that she could see above her was the underside of the landing of the second floor. However, she quickly realised that it wasn't banging and scratching she could hear, but rather more of a metallic clattering, and it was coming from below her.

'Come on, this is the last lot! The passage is being blown in five minutes! The Prussians are almost through!'

It took a moment for the meaning of the shout to register with Kitty, but when it did it was like the shot of adrenaline that raced through her body every time she entered combat. Her brain snapped into focus as new energy infused her limbs and she pushed herself away from the wall, filled with a new determination. She promptly tangled herself up in the crutches and very nearly came a cropper, only just catching herself before she fell headlong down the stairs by throwing herself back against the wall.

'More haste less waste, Kitty.' She mumbled to herself as she tried again.

Negotiating the steps down, even though they were quite wide at the outside of the wide staircase, was a much harder task than the flat corridor and even with her renewed vitality it was slow and very hard going. She managed to get a fairly good rhythm going once she worked out that she had to put the crutches on the step below her first, though.

The clattering noise had gone, along with the shouting, but when she was almost in sight of the next landing it returned.

'Come on! Come on! Hurry it up! Two minutes!'

She came around the bend of the stairwell just in time to see the last of a group of medical personnel come out of the wards on that floor, pushing wheelchairs. The patients in them hung on for dear life as they were banged down the low steps by the running men and women and it was a miracle that they didn't tumble head over heels. She hobbled across the landing to the banister as quickly as she could, intending to call down to them, but they were already out of sight around the bend when she got there and the only trace left of them was the echoing of the abused wheelchairs.

'Damn it.'

Two minutes. There was only one flight to go, but even that was too far and she wouldn't make it in only two minutes, especially because her body was on the point of giving up the ghost - dark blobs were floating across her eyes and her limbs were becoming numb. She had set her mind on escaping, though, so she wasn't about to give up. Plus, if she'd learnt one thing from the British it was not to abandon hope in the face of an apparently impossible situation - if they had, Britain would probably have ceased to exist in 1940.

She hobbled to the top of the stairs and started down, moving much faster than before, almost recklessly, in an effort to get to the bottom in time. The deeper she had gone, the more the noise of the Prussians digging had faded and, apart from the knocking of her crutches against the floor, the hospital was completely silent now that the clatter of the wheelchairs had ended. That was bad, because it meant everybody had gone, but it also meant that they hadn't blown up the passageway, and until they did that, she had a chance.

Half-way down the stairs, disaster struck. The foot of one of the crutches slipped on an ancient and worn stone and she overbalanced. There was no way for her to catch herself and she tumbled face first down the stairs. She tried to curl up to protect herself, but her bad leg wouldn't obey and all she could really do was wrap her hands around her head and hope for the best.

She rolled over and over, screaming in agony. The fall seemed to last an eternity, but finally she came to a rest and lay face down on the cold stone gasping for breath and fighting to retain consciousness.

Her vision was blurred, but she could just about make out that she was all the way down at the bottom of the stairs. She could also see the wall where the hidden passageway was supposed to be.

There was no sign of the hidden door - it was closed.

After all her effort. After enduring the pain of moving to get down the stairs. After the final sprint that had sent her spinning out of control and crashing to the ground. After *all* that she was too late - the undersea boat would leave and Gruber would get her. Or at least what was left of her.

'I thought I heard something! I just want to take a look!'

A section of the wall opposite her ground open and a face poked out into the hallway. For a moment, Kitty thought she was hallucinating, but then the door opened more and a figure ran towards her.

'She's here!'

As the figure came closer it resolved into the familiar shape of Polly. She grabbed Kitty's arm and began trying to tug her towards the opening in the wall, but she wasn't able to shift her; she was just too much of a dead weight for the girl.

'I can't...' Polly was in tears and her voice cracked with frustration. 'You've got to help me, Kitty!'

Kitty moaned and made a supreme effort to do as she was asked, knowing it was her last chance to make it to the boat, but there was no strength left in her and her arms barely shifted an inch.

'Just leave...'

Suddenly there were two men there as well. They pushed Polly roughly to the side, then picked Kitty up between them and sprinted for the opening.

'You owe us, Polly.'

'Anything, Tris, anything. Thank you.'

The two men got Kitty through the doorway and bundled her into a wheelchair, waiting just inside. While the two men swung the door closed behind them, Polly grabbed the handles of the wheelchair and began pushing. After only a few paces the chair was going at a fair clip, aided by the slight slope of the passageway.

Kitty barely had the presence of mind to hold on as she rocked back and forth and was only vaguely aware of the two men running behind them. She didn't notice when they stopped, but she certainly did when they caught up with them again, because their shouts were deafening in her ears.

'Fire in the hole!'

The small group went around a bend in the passageway at breakneck speed and Kitty's wheelchair went up on one wheel. It would have overturned if one of the men hadn't grabbed it and slammed it back down. Even then they didn't slow, but after only a few paces, there was a booming roar from behind them and then a deep rumble as the passageway filled with dust.

'You can slow down now, Polly. We're safe.'

'Thanks, Tris. Thanks, Willie.'

The two men grinned at Polly, then nodded at Kitty, however, while the young woman slowed to a walk, they continued to jog down the slope.

Kitty craned her head to look back at Polly. She was so different to the girl who she and Gwen had met only months before during the evacuation of Muscovy by the Misfits, with a determination and a maturity to her that made her seem so much older than her twenty-odd years. It made Kitty wonder just how much she had been through in her time on the island, how much she had seen. It had been a trial for everyone, but working in the hospital must have been a hellish nightmare.

Polly felt Kitty's gaze on her and glanced down at her. A wide grin temporarily smoothed out the lines on her forehead and banished the worry from her eyes, giving Kitty a glimpse of the girl that still lurked beneath the serious outer shell.

'Sorry about the bumpy ride. We're almost there now, though, just a few more yards. How are you feeling?'

'Like I've been shot, thrown down a flight of stairs, then rolled down a hill by a maniac.'

Polly chuckled. 'I've seen you look worse. We'll get you checked out as soon as we get on board and make sure that nothing got shook loose on the trip down.'

'Thank you.'

They went around a sharp turn in the passageway and suddenly it opened up into a large cavern, filled with water. Sitting in the middle of the wide pool, against a wooden jetty, was a big grey undersea boat, its conning tower reaching almost to the roughly hewn ceiling. The last of the sick and injured were just being lowered down through the various hatches in the top of its hull by sailors and Polly pushed the wheelchair along the jetty towards the nearest group.

Kitty eyed the boat warily. She didn't really like the idea of being trapped inside the metal tube, unable to see the sky or breathe fresh air.

'So, how long will it take us to get to England?'

Polly shook her head. 'We're not going all the way to England. They can only take us as far as Gibraltar.'

'Oh.'

'Don't worry, we'll be in Gibraltar in a few days and I know a really good pub we can hang around in while you wait for transport. You won't have a chance to miss Gwen, I'll make sure of it!'

As two sailors pulled her out of the wheelchair and lifted her bodily into the hatch, Kitty smiled at the girl. 'I'm sure you will.'

The Misfits would likely be in England already and Kitty didn't fancy being stuck in Gibraltar, waiting for a transport, any more than she wanted to be shut up in the undersea boat for any length of time; there were too many bad memories there. However, it was one step closer to Gwen. And that was all that mattered.

ABOUT THE AUTHOR

Simon Brading's interest in aviation began when he was very young and at thirteen he joined the RAF section of the Combined Cadet Forces of Dulwich College with the aim of becoming a pilot. However, when he was 18, had reached the rank of Flight Sergeant in the CCF and was trying to get into a University Air Squadron, he was told that his eyesight wasn't good enough to be a pilot, so he had to move onto plan B... something else.

He tried his hand at many things before it occurred to him that he might have a few stories to tell. He never lost his interest in flight, though, and hopes to add a PPL to his very basic and probably extremely expired glider license.

www.simonbrading.co.uk

For news of special offers, upcoming releases, exclusive content, competitions and events, please follow me on social media.

Instagram - @sibrading
Facebook - Simon Brading Author
Tiktok - @SimonBradingAuthor

In addition, souvenirs and merchandise, including T-shirts, badges, stickers and more, are available from the Misfit Squadron store on REDBUBBLE at
https://www.redbubble.com/people/misfitsquadron/shop

ALSO BY SIMON BRADING

The "Displacers" series - a young adult time travel adventure series for all ages.
The Time Traveller's Nephew
The Secret of the Ancients
The Whitechapel Plot
The Price of Greed
The Time for Vengeance

The "Misfit Squadron" Series - a Steampunk series set in an alternate World War 2.
The Battle Over Britain
The Russian Resistance
A Misfit Midwinter
The Lion and the Baron
The Maltese Defence
Tales From the Second Great War
The Siege of Gibraltar
The King's Mission
The Home Front

The Dismal Futures books - stand-alone science fiction tales suitable for adults.
Empath
The Lifeboat at the End of the Universe

The "Twin Ambitions" series - ballet books for children ages 7 and up.
Fight to Dance
Back to Basics

The "Ni Hon - The Two Books" Series - a young adult series set in a dystopian future Japan.
The Black Book

Others
Public Enemy